OLDER HOTTER GRUMPIER

EVIE ROSE

Copyright © 2023 by Evie Rose

All rights reserved.

No part of this book may be reproduced in any form or by any electronic or mechanical means, including information storage and retrieval systems, without written permission from the author, except for the use of brief quotations in a book review.

This story is a work of fiction. Names, characters, places, and incidents are the product of the author's imagination or are used fictitiously. Any resemblance to actual events, locales, or persons, living or dead, is coincidental.

Cover: © 2023 by Evie Rose. Images under licence from Deposit Photos.

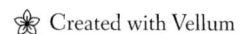

❀ Created with Vellum

1

ELLA

By twenty-three, some people already have babies, houses with cute gardens, jobs with humorous bosses, and loving alien husbands.

I'm not jealous. Much.

Wait, mostly not the alien thing.

I click around on my computer screen, totally unable to focus on work. My severe and gorgeous billionaire boss is out for the whole afternoon, as he is every Wednesday. In his absence, my brain is refusing to do anything but think about the book I was reading. Which isn't normal for me. I know it's pathetic, but I'm desperate to please my grumpy boss.

When he's here, as his assistant I ensure everything is perfect, in the hopes that one day I will earn a smile from him. Sure, a little bit because he's demanding, but also because I adore him, surly temper, grey morals, and all.

I guess it's because sometimes when he looks out of the window of this skyscraper office, he seems so lonely. Like he's the only person on this planet.

I get that. Every day of the week and literally all of

Sundays. Well, except the weekends when Mr Blackwood sends me a terse email asking if I can work overtime, and I leave my tiny room in a shared apartment and weekend to-be-read pile with tragic speed.

But this afternoon? I'm alone in this echoey office and I've stuffed the gap with the only thing—other than Mr Blackwood—that comforts me: reading.

The book I started at lunchtime is rioting in my head. It hooked me good. The story is that the curvy heroine is selected for an alien breeding program, and the seven-foot-tall blue alien with a special peen turns up at her workplace —she's an office bunny like me—and drags her away to his spaceship for a week of bonding. They've just had the first day, when he gets to lick her wherever he likes. And he does like, believe me. They've had the sweet scene where he charms her despite being massive and grumpy and, well. Blue.

But, plot twist, another group of aliens is trying to steal her because human women are so desirable, so she and her blue hero are on the run across a desert planet.

I'm absolutely desperate to read the next part, which has been teased as when they'll get it on. It's going to be hot.

I just know there will be the cutest baby epilogue and I cannot wait for that either.

But can I? Nooooo.

Born to read, forced to work.

I wish an alien who wanted to breed and adore and comfort me would select me as his mate. Why do all the best things happen to fictional characters, and not me?

I glance up at my boss' closed door, empty behind it. My appreciation for the blue alien romance hero has nothing to do with him. Nothing.

Mr Blackwood has these bubble-gum blue eyes, so

bright you'd think they were fake, but I've studied them. They're not contacts or anything like that, he's just ludicrously genetically blessed. He has soft-looking dark brown hair with a slight curl and a hint of silver at his temples. He always wears a crisp navy suit and a silk tie. He's not seven feet tall, but he might as well be. He towers above me and makes me feel as dainty as a fairy.

When he's not being a growly bear, that is.

Mr Blackwood is the terror of the company, and not just because we all know this firm cleans money for his mafia. It's an open secret since he threatened to dump his previous assistant in a canal. Which was fine until he actually was discovered drowned in a river. Sudden interest in cold water swimming. Apparently.

Though that has never scared me.

Nope. Mr Blackwood is perfect, so it's understandable that he's the most demanding boss and intolerant of failure.

Why he keeps me as his secretary, god only knows, because all he ever does is criticise my spelling and make me stay late to redo things.

But Mr Blackwood has a sweet side. He insists on driving me home when I have to work into the evening, which is most days. And when he emails me on the weekend asking me to do overtime, he gives me a lift to the office. I always spot him waiting in a luxurious car outside my apartment after I say I'm available. I've decided it is him being protective of me as a member of his staff, but there are other interpretations.

Like, I hope I don't suddenly find an interest in cold water swimming.

But Mr Blackwood is out for his weekly Wednesday afternoon mystery outing. He won't return until after five or tomorrow morning, and won't say where he was.

I screwed up my courage and asked once, and received a terse, "None of your business", in reply.

Probably he just plays golf, but I can't help thinking that the discipline with which he keeps this appointment makes it something more. He's so intense and work focused the rest of the time that Wednesday afternoon feels out of character to be a hobby.

My curiosity about my hot boss' activities aside, he'll never know I wasn't staring at spreadsheets, but words about spread legs on silk sheets.

I slide my phone discreetly from my pocket, stealthy, though unscheduled interruptions to Mr Blackwood's whole top floor office are far fewer now.

Mr Blackwood doesn't like being disturbed, even I can see that. Yes, he's totally capable of snarling at visitors himself—talented at it in fact—but people are constantly trying to get Mr Blackwood's time, money, or attention.

My gamble was that he didn't like having to growl in person. So however insistent, bulky, loaded with firearms under their neat suits, or irritated at the short blonde girl guarding her boss a caller is, unless they have an appointment, they can leave a message or send an email.

I deliver all this with a charming smile, of course.

And it has made it peaceful on the top floor. Just me and him.

Balancing my phone on the bottom of my computer screen, I flick my gaze to the elevator. My desk is in a light-filled entrance that leads to Mr Blackwood's office. I'm the dragon in a dress who guards my boss. Keeper of his diary, provider of his tea, listener of his grumps.

But my role means anyone might walk into my workplace at any moment. No need to knock. And it would be the worst to be caught reading—especially something this spicy—on work time.

I angle my body and the phone so I'm facing the elevator, my back to Mr Blackwood's door. That's safe, since he's out. And then with shaking hands, I open the eBook app.

As I read, a grin creeps across my face.

Oh this is perfect. They're stuck in a cave, waiting out a sandstorm that is protecting them from the bad guys who are after her, because human women who can be bred are so unusual. The tension is extreme. He makes a comment about how she thinks she's too good for an alien king like him, and she goes to disagree, then in the dark, they find each other. The hero kisses the heroine and—this is my favourite trope—is telling her she's pretty. That he wants to breed her so badly. That he can't wait to fill her up with his seed.

Between my legs is liquid heat as I read. Why do none of the men I date say things like this? Maybe if they did, I wouldn't still be a virgin.

Oh right. I forgot.

I don't date.

Who needs dating when you have blue alien book boyfriends to say, "You're going to take my big cock so well"?

I press my thighs together in a vain attempt to get the pressure I so desperately want on my clit.

In the book, he's lifting her onto his lap and telling her she's the most beautiful thing he's ever seen.

I'm ridiculously turned on. I'm squirming. I need…

As I keep reading, the beat between my legs thrums harder, demanding. I'm so wet. It wouldn't take long to come when I'm this horny. It would be almost instant.

Glancing up, I bite my lip.

Dare I?

Really?

I'd be in so much trouble if I got caught. But I would hear the elevator clunk to a stop before the doors opened and anyone could see into my foyer office. I'd be able to whip my phone down and be typing productively in seconds.

I creep my hand into my lap.

The desk is massive and solid wood. No one can see what I'm doing from the elevator side.

And although I tell myself it's safe, I admit, it feels the hottest sort of naughty to slowly drag the hem of my dress up and slip my fingers underneath. The taboo is making this far sexier than any workplace should be. My knickers are soaked. That book is very steamy, and as my fingertips brush the fabric, I bite back a moan. I'm utterly on edge.

I know I'm about to come hard.

I push the cotton aside and sparks shower my body as I touch my clit. I moan.

"Miss Button."

My head snaps around, my hand flies out from my knickers, and my heart tries to throw itself out of my mouth.

My boss is standing *behind* me. *Watching*.

"Mr Blackwood," I squawk at a pitch so high it's probably only audible to dogs, and scramble to hide my activities, bumping my mouse to get my screen on, knocking my phone flat. So doing, my elbow catches the pot full of bright glitter pens and they clatter all over the desk, cascading onto the floor.

I throw myself after them, banging my knees in my haste. The plush carpet softens my fall, and I grab at the pens blindly. I was so focused on people coming through the elevator door, it never occurred to me to check whether my boss was *in*.

Silent as a shadow, he's immediately there, kneeling beside me, a solid rock of calm in my messy sea. He reaches for a blue pen as I flush even redder and try to snatch it up. With the inevitability of a train crash, I grab his hand then retract as though burnt.

Oh my god, those are the fingers I was using to touch myself. I just put my girl come onto my billionaire mafia boss' knuckles.

"Sorry," I blurt.

I'm going to die. He might have me murdered, but it's far more likely I will spontaneously combust with humiliation. My skin flames.

I'm in actual hell. Only explanation. I've already died, I died of shock the second Mr Blackwood said my name. My cheeks are being toasted by some snide little devil of the underworld, saying like, "You fancied your boss, didn't you? And now he's seen you reading smut and revealing your virginal white knickers. You died with your V-card, ha!"

I sneak a look at Mr Blackwood when he doesn't reply. He's looking at me strangely, his blue eyes dark as a late summer evening.

But as he rises, he adjusts his trousers.

Is he...? Surely not.

"Miss Button, you're flushed," he says, and his voice is at its coldest.

Oh no. I'm going to be sacked for sure.

I think I might cry. My bottom lip is legit wobbling as I get to my feet, keeping my gaze lowered like I'm a toddler denied a sweet treat for being naughty. Except, I'm twenty-three, and the indulgence is *seeing my boss every day*, and the bad behaviour is *flicking the bean at work while reading alien smut.*

How have I never noticed how much better this thick blue carpet is than anything else in the room? Good carpet. Nice carpet. My friend. Gah.

"Look at me."

With the reluctance of a cat going outside in the rain, I lift my head to my boss' face.

I'm drowning in his eyes. Like. Dying. Surrounded and pressurised by the blue. Sinking under the water and unable to breathe.

"We need to discuss this, Miss Button. My office. Now."

2

RAFE

If I'd known all I had to do was remain quietly in the office to see my sweet little young assistant slipping her fingers into her knickers, I'd have fucking slept here for the past eighteen months. I'd have never left.

I thought I had no honour remaining after being a mafia boss of Sutton for twenty years. My brothers and I competed and fought and supported each other to the top of two of London's mafias and another in Milan. I sold my soul to money and power long ago. But apparently even I cannot watch a woman seventeen years younger than me, and my employee, touch herself and not announce my presence.

Fucking honour. I should have just enjoyed the show. It's all I'll ever get.

She's going to want to leave. It's baffling she's remained as my secretary since I've been painfully obvious I cannot stand even twenty-four hours without seeing her. Talking with her. Simply being near her and knowing she's safe is enough some nights when I stay in my SUV outside her building.

My excuses are thin at the best of times. I've portrayed

myself as an entitled bastard, demanding that she type my emails and read my memos aloud. I think she assumes I'm dyslexic, when in actual fact the world is bleak without her. And now I've made it uncomfortable, which makes me want to roar and tear shit up, because she has never been awkward with me.

I sink into my black leather chair and Miss Button slinks into the office, hovering by the exit as though she might bolt. She's still flushed, but she's also scared.

My little sunshine dragon. She doesn't need to be afraid of me. She certainly isn't of anyone else. Where every assistant before her has been happy to let me deal with any annoyances, Miss Button understood from the start.

I heard her first. Her voice is upbeat, chirpy. But when any of my useless previous assistants would have phoned through and asked if I would see the visitor, she stood firm, repeating that if I had blocked out time without meetings with "do not disturb", that she wouldn't allow me to be disturbed for less than a life-or-death crisis.

Admittedly, they're more common than she imagines in my line of work, but I appreciated the gesture.

And she did it all with a sweet smile.

That was when I got into the habit of watching my assistant. There's a CCTV camera hidden in her foyer office, which I think is fine. The one in her building, where I can keep an eye on her comings and goings, I feel a bit more ambiguous about. I definitely shouldn't have a tracker on her phone, but how else can I be sure she is home safely?

"Close the door, Miss Button."

I don't call her Ella—such a sweet name—because I dare not risk the barrier of professionalism between us. Though having watched her drag her skirt up might have blown that out of the water. Even more than me moaning her name and picturing her face being splattered with my come as I jerk myself off in the shower every morning.

She hesitates before closing the door with a click. The silence here is normally a haven, but right now it's stifling.

And it's not helping that I have no fucking idea what I'm going to say. The things flying around my mind are wildly inappropriate, even given the terms that we're working on since I caught her flicking the bean.

Get to your knees and open your mouth.

Bend over and prepare to be spanked like the naughty girl you are.

Come here, pull up your skirt, and sit on my cock.

Next time you want to come, you ask me.

My little assistant though? She has it covered. Taking quick strides across the room, she stops before my desk. Back straight, she clasps her hands together before her.

"Please don't sack me." She's trembling. "My mother already thinks I'm a waste of space."

Her mother *what*? "Want me to kill her?"

"No!" If it's possible, she's even more flustered. "She's my mother!"

I shrug. Anyone who upsets my girl should die. End of.

"Just please, please let me keep my job," she begs.

She's really serious. She thinks I'm going to fire her. I guess I'm so much older it hasn't occurred to her that after seeing her touch herself I'm far more inclined to lay her on my desk and fuck her until she cries. For mercy or because she's coming for the fourth time, I can't decide. Both?

There's nothing she could do to make me let her go. She could murder the entire marketing department and I'd shake my head and tell HR to get on the job of replacing them. Quickly, in case she decided to unalive them too.

"Please."

Poor sad girl.

I didn't have a particular game in mind when I called her into my office. But it occurs to me now I can use this situation to my advantage. Sure, it's immoral, but who said I had morals? I stopped being ethical at the same time as I stopped eating my food pureed on a spoon.

"What would you do to keep your job, Miss Button?"

"Anything." Her voice is steady on that word, and she meets my eyes.

Brave little sunshine dragon. She has no idea what she's saying.

"Be my date for an event this evening."

Her jaw drops open. "A fake date."

After wanting her for eighteen months, no. A *real* date. "Yes."

Because however much I long to have this woman on my dick, there are some major issues we can't overcome. In particular: she's way too young for me, she's my assistant, she's sweet and innocent where I am sour and jaded.

But one night of having her by my side at this godforsaken charity event I wish I'd never started? Abso-fucking-lutely. It never used to bother me that there were so many proud parents at this thing. Then when I met Ella, seeing happy couples and cute kids became torture. How is it fair that all those men have loving wives and have bred talented children, and I only have a billion in the bank and two annoying brothers who won't allow me to forget where we came from: the gutter.

So yeah, even if it's a con, I'll take it.

She licks her lips as she thinks about this proposal. It's a good one, surely? Hardly inappropriate at all. In a relative sense. Compared to say, fucking my assistant over my desk.

I'll have an evening of indulging in her by my side, her

hand in mine, my palm at the small of her back guiding her. I'll have my fill of limited, casually intimate touches. I'll brush the blonde hair from her eyes and tuck it behind her ear. I'll wrap my arm around her waist, pull her close, and kiss the top of her head.

For one night, we'll pretend.

"But why do you need a fake date?" she asks, straightening her shoulders. "You could have any woman you liked."

"I don't want any of those women." I want *her*. Ella.

"And they get tedious, I suppose, throwing themselves at you," she continues.

I nod, because since I met Ella the thought of being with anyone else has left me cold. Compared to my vibrant assistant, my cock says meh.

She has this bright energy that matches her sunshine hair and smile and I want to bathe in it every time I see her. She's a walking light box and eases the seasonal affective disorder that I get in all four seasons. Anytime she's not here.

"So I'll run interference." She perks up. "Just like when we're at work, I'll protect you from unwanted attention, because you don't need women fawning over you."

I nod slowly, because if that's how she wants to justify this to herself, sure.

"One evening of being your fake date, and we'll forget that... Incident... Ever happened?"

"If that's what you prefer," I reply evenly. Hopefully the possessive monster in my chest will be satisfied, and she can continue being my assistant while I live off the memories.

She lets out a shaky breath, like she's been holding it. "Okay. Okay, thank you, Mr Blackwood."

"Rafe."

She swallows and repeats my name softly. "Rafe."

And hell, that makes my cock twitch. It pleases me that she calls me Mr Blackwood, or boss. But Rafe? That's special. Not an honorific, or something any of my men would call me.

"Where shall I meet—"

"I'll pick you up at seven." I'm already counting the minutes until I can justify touching her.

"Right." There's that anxiety again. "And the dress code?"

Oh, this has potential I hadn't realised. Not just a girlfriend. No. Nothing so commonplace for my girl. "Everything for you to wear will be provided."

"But the size—"

"It will be the right size," I assure her. It will be, or someone will be shot.

She smiles shyly. And like with every sunshine smile she gives me, my heart seizes up my whole body. I can't do anything but watch her from beneath lowered brows.

If I was a better man, one who deserved her and was at least a decade younger, I would return that smile. I'd tell her that from the moment she walked into my office that first day, I was transfixed by her. Her smile. Her mouth. The cascade of blonde hair that she always has in a swishy ponytail.

I'd find her a new job and take her on real dates.

Instead, I'm me. Covered by a black shadow of my own deeds and bad temper, on the edge of giving up or burning everything to the ground most days. Until my sunshine dragon gave me something to live for.

She must be used to my lack of response, because after a beat, she turns to go.

"I'll get back to work," she murmurs. "Thank—"

"Wait."

She halts instantly. My cock, which has been chubby throughout this conversation, swells.

This is the problem. Her doing what I tell her—and she does that excellently—makes my cock impossibly hard. Painfully.

Her glance over her shoulder is wary, like I could withdraw my offer. No chance. I might never let her out of my sight.

"Don't you want to finish reading your book?"

3

ELLA

It's a trick question. That's my first thought. If this were anyone else—like my mother—I'd assume it was a game and they were about to laugh at me if I say, yes, I do want to read my book.

After all, it was at a really good bit.

But Mr Blackwood doesn't laugh. He doesn't smile or make snide comments. He's a grump, and while he's dangerous and powerful, I've never seen him be less than straightforward. I'm honest with him, and he's honest with me. I reckon that's how I'm still here when usually his assistants last about two months. So either this is far more cruel than I expect from him, or...

"Don't you want to know how it ends?" he adds.

"Yes," I admit. "But I'll read it tonight. I'm supposed to be working now."

"You'll be *busy* later," he replies smoothly.

When did the word busy become so utterly filthy? It must be just in my head. My boss has already been beyond generous. He hasn't sacked me, when literally anyone would have done.

He caught me touching my *pussy* at work. At my desk.

"You don't want me to read the rest of my book on work time." It's not exactly a question, but neither is it a statement.

"Isn't that what you were going to do if I wasn't here?" he replies dryly.

I wince. "Maybe?"

"Well." He gestures to the couch across from him in the spacious office. "Far be it from me to prevent you from finishing."

There's an emphasis on that last word that makes my cheeks heat. Honestly, I've blushed so much this afternoon I must have a lack of blood anywhere else in my body. Specifically, my brain and my knees. And that's how I account for the fact that I don't protest about being a professional, or say I don't want to read my book.

Nope. With a feeling of weightlessness, like I might drift into space any second, I go to the leather sofa he has indicated, and sit.

I slipped my phone into the pocket of my work dress as I followed Mr Blackwood into his office—didn't want anyone else seeing it—and I pull it out.

Under his watchful gaze, the device pings right back to the page I was reading when I open it.

The words that just seemed sexy and fun earlier have suddenly taken on new significance when reading them in my boss' office.

I'm nervous, tingling all over from how naughty this is—reading porn in front of my silver fox older boss—even as I do as I'm told, and read to the bottom of the page, barely taking in the meaning.

"Good girl."

I glance up, but Mr Blackwood doesn't acknowledge

that he's said that to me—was it even to me?—he's concentrating on his computer.

Good girl. I really, really want that. To be *his* good girl. He's called me that only once before. When I first arrived as his assistant, and I defended his closed door as ferociously as a puppy with a forbidden sock.

Good girl. It melts me.

So I return to reading, as he instructed. And it takes a few minutes, but the story ensnares me, drawing me back in. It's smutty and soft and intimate, keeping me turning the pages even as I continue to glance up at Mr Blackwood every minute, like my mind wants to check this is really happening.

The hero caresses the heroine everywhere. Lays her down and licks her. Makes her come on his tongue. And then finally, finally, she crawls onto his lap and asks him to breed her.

It's so hot I can barely breathe. I press my thighs together. Subtly. It sends a tiny bolt of pleasure through my body, so small as to be unsatisfying but better than nothing, so I do it again. A little movement. And again.

Mr Blackwood isn't looking at me. There's just the slight clicks of his mouse and the swoosh of his arm in that white shirt.

My clit doesn't care that he isn't watching. It's throbbing from the combination of this book and being close to my sexy boss.

"You're squirming, Miss Button."

I freeze.

"I am?" I ask in a little voice, as though I'm somehow not aware that I've been trying to get some pressure on my clit.

"Why don't you do it?" he rumbles.

"What?" I'm not understanding this conversation, too fogged from reading this book and from the sensation of his knowing presence.

"You know." He turns his head slowly towards me and raises his eyebrows. "What you normally do when you read a book like that."

"How..." I was going to ask how he knows what kind of book it is, but... Yeah. Okay. He saw what I was about to do. He knows what sort of book this is.

At least he doesn't know all that stuff about blue eyes, and a massive cock, and breeding... The thought of him knowing I like reading that, and making inferences—correctly—about what I daydream about... This time I can't even pretend the blush is pure embarrassment. It's not. It's arousal that makes my nipples peak.

"Lift your skirt, Miss Button."

Like I'm his puppet, my hands go to the hem of my dress. The dress is soft as it drags up my thighs.

He's watching me intently.

I pause when the bunched fabric would reveal my white cotton underwear, reluctant to show him. He's sophisticated and wealthy, and I'm... Just me. In my normal panties with my boring self. I'm his toy.

And that thought makes my clit twitch.

His toy.

I had no idea I had this kink.

"Go on," he croons. "Exactly as you were going to do earlier. Ignore me." Leaning back, he slides his hand into his lap and my imagination fills in the gaps as I hear a rustle. Is he hard?

Heart hammering, I push my hand under my dress and let out a little whine as my fingers rub against the cotton.

"That's it. Touch yourself."

I'm helpless to do anything other than what he directs. My knickers are soaking.

"Are you wet, my pretty girl?"

Nodding, I writhe. Am I his pretty girl? I'd love to ask, but I'm afraid of the answer. That it's just a casual word, and doesn't mean anything. I'd rather stick with my fantasy that I'm his good girl, his pretty girl. As in. *His.*

Pressing my clit through the cotton, pleasure flares out.

"Let me see."

It must be the lure of his voice, because I slide my skirt further up, revealing my knickers in all their plain, virginal not-glory.

Mr Blackwood nods. "Very good. My good girl. I can see them glistening. Now part your legs and reach inside for me."

He's utterly motionless and controlled as I'm writhing, unleashed and needy. I thought that my book was hot? It was nothing compared to my boss telling me what to do.

I let my knees fall apart and slip my hand into my knickers, and down until I reach slick moisture first, then the soft folds of my sex. I've done this plenty of times over the last eighteen months—touch myself and think of Mr Blackwood—but it's never felt like this. Not so vivid. It's like I've lived everything up until now on a cloudy day, and suddenly Mr Blackwood has shoved me into the dazzling sunshine.

Every movement of my fingers over my clit is a hundred times bigger than it ever has been before. I circle where I'm most sensitive. There's no resistance, only my hand stretching out the white cotton.

There's a soft groan from the other side of the room. It's Mr Blackwood.

"Does that feel good?" he says, low and gravelly.

"Yes," I pant out.

"You're such a brave girl. Anyone could walk in and see you being so filthy. My naughty secretary, touching yourself in my office."

A sob escapes me. Being seen? Who knew it was such a scorching fantasy.

"Are you close? Your cheeks are flushed. So pretty. You're doing so well," he tells me.

I keen, unable to form words. I'm right on the edge.

"I can smell you from here."

A pulse goes through my clit, and I don't know if it's his voice, or the electric embarrassment of this whole situation.

He raises his hand to his mouth, rubbing the dark stubble on his jaw, then goes shock still.

Yes. Oh. Oh no. Because simultaneously we both have the same realisation.

I touched his hand with the fingers that had been in my pussy.

Holding my gaze, my boss tilts his big square wrist and brings his knuckles to his nose before taking a deep breath in.

"Mmmm. Delicious."

I let out a squeak of pure arousal. Of need. And my boss? He lowers his hand just enough so I can see him open his mouth and slowly lick the place where my fingers brushed.

That lick echoes through my body as strongly as if it had been my skin. Maybe more.

I explode. I think I cry out. I definitely shudder as I come so hard I see stars in burst after burst. They start from my pussy but reach right down to my toes. It's a whole-body drug, this orgasm. It's magic on a scale I've never felt.

He doesn't take his greedy eyes from me as I arch and

shake and lose all sense of time and place, even as the spasms slowly ebb away.

Oh. My. God. I just—

There's a tap on the door.

"Mr Blackwood?" a tentative voice says, and then babbles. "There is a delivery for you, Mr Blackwood, but your secretary isn't here, and I didn't know what to do."

"One moment please," Mr Blackwood orders. He takes his time to stand, still not having taken his eyes off me, and adjusts his trousers over the obvious bulge at the front, with no shame whatsoever.

My brain unsticks and I scramble to get my clothes straight as he strolls to the door. Jumping to wobbly feet, I push down my dress and, blushing again, look, horrified, at my sticky fingers.

Caught with my hand in the honey pot. Literally.

The options fly through my head as Mr Blackwood waits. Wipe them on my dress, or my knickers. Stuff my hands in my pockets, or put them balled behind my back—I very nearly do that. Then I think of how my fingers brushed Mr Blackwood's accidentally. And instead, I do what my eight-year-old self said was the best way to get rid of evidence.

Eat it.

Shoving my fingers into my mouth I suck the liquid off as fast as I can, the tart, salt and sweet hitting the back of my throat. Then I rub my fingers into my palms and clasp my hands together in front of me.

The very picture of innocence.

I hope.

Something flares in Mr Blackwood's gaze.

"That was very well done," he says, low and for my ears only. "Good girl."

Ohhhh... I melt. Sure, he's said that before, and yeah, I melt every time. But right now? What does he mean? The cover-up, or what came before? I don't have the opportunity to ask, as he pulls open the door wide, revealing a harassed-looking receptionist and a stack of at least ten large packages, including several dress bags.

I goggle at the pile and look at Mr Blackwood.

And I swear, my grumpy boss, for the first time since I have known him, smirks.

4

RAFE

I'm outside her apartment before seven. Fuck, I'm eager as a teenage boy to see her, and begin our evening together.

Watch her come again, too. Surely I can persuade her to do that? Then it's just a skip and a jump to being my wife and having my children. Simple.

Ella touching herself was so insanely hot. I've never seen anything as beautiful as her face overtaken by pleasure.

I'd say that was the best thing I'll ever see, but I know having her closer, on my cock, coming from me stroking her and thrusting into her, would be even better.

She might have gotten off on the taboo of wanking in the office, but I'm still her older boss. Need to invest in one of those age-reversal cons. Maybe time travel? Whatever it would take to convince Ella that she's meant to be with me.

In the absence of implausible technology, I'm currently thinking of numerous orgasms, spoiling her rotten, and getting her used to the idea of being my bride by the very subtle means of pretending we're already in a relationship. Maybe she just won't notice if I never stop?

It's a dark, cold, crisp winter's evening and above the

blue-orange glow of London's lights, there are stars as I decide it doesn't matter if I'm early, I'm going to get my girl, when she emerges from the front door.

I'm sent flying.

Not literally, but I might as well be. Ella is wearing the dress I chose for her, a long silky purple thing that takes my breath away. Her blonde hair is down in waves over her shoulders and my imagination leaps right to that hair wrapped around my fist.

She's the most beautiful woman I've ever seen.

I approach in swift steps, unable to wait patiently, and she gives me that tentative smile. "You were right. It fit."

Of course it did. I've spent enough time looking at her to be sure of every measurement... Some might say stalking her. Following her home on the few days I don't drive her myself. Sitting outside her apartment, sometimes all night. "Do you like it?"

She bites her bottom lip and nods, and my cock throbs.

It's all I can do to help her into the car like a gentleman rather than unleash the beast raging beneath my skin. It's pure possessive instinct.

"Do I look okay?" she asks as the limo pulls away.

"You look almost perfect."

"I'll take it," she replies sheepishly. "I do my best, but—"

"I won't."

"Oh." Her face drops. "Sorry, I can—"

I grab her chin between my thumb and forefinger, and tilt her face up to mine. Such big eyes. She's the most delicious little morsel and I want to eat her up, cunt first.

"I don't date."

"No. I understand." But she doesn't, because she looks sad and confused. "I won't do anything to commit you. You're a powerful billionaire boss—"

"Ella. Secrets." It's public knowledge, but no one says it about the more refined mafias of London. It's a taboo that can get you killed. It nearly did get me killed once or twice when I was Ella's age.

"Yes, boss."

"Good girl." She smiles shyly and my heart beats like percussion as I draw the box from my jacket pocket and present it to her. Small, black. Obviously a ring box. "This is what is missing from your outfit."

There's a flash of panic on her face and I flip open the box.

"I can't wear that!" she protests, but goes to touch it anyway.

"Why not?"

"Everyone will think..." She licks her lips, leaving them shiny, and kissable. Or fuckable.

"Ella. I told you. I don't date. Everyone will think whatever they like. This way, you'll be convincing."

"That's... True."

I pluck the ring out and toss the box aside, taking Ella's small hand in mine. She stretches out her fingers and there's a velvet silence as I slide the band onto her finger.

The relief when she accepts my ring is as strong as that time the Camden mafia stopped pulling my fingernails out. And when she twists her wrist so she can admire it, a pleased little smile twitching her lips, that's magical.

"I love it. Thank you."

"No more than what you deserve." I should have been spoiling her twenty-four hours a day since we met.

She makes a modest, equivocal noise. "Where are we going?"

Ahhh.

I didn't think this through.

"A charity event." I wonder if I can avoid her meeting my brother? I can really do without him spilling the whole story of how we were penniless orphans, blah blah blah, climbed our way up from nothing, so dull. Sev and I control the parts of London most mafias consider beneath them. Ridiculous.

"Oh?" She peppers me with questions about the charity, which I evade. I've been her boss, the influential mafia boss. What will she think if she discovers I was a rejected kid, and I spend every Wednesday teaching art at my old school like an absolute sap?

Far too soon, we arrive at the upscale hotel I hired for the evening. There's intimidation in Ella's gaze as she takes in the impressive facade and bright lights, even before the flashes of paparazzi cameras pop.

"Are you sure about this?" she says in a tone of panic as I get out of the car and go to open her door. There is a crowd milling around outside the hotel, and she looks up at me when I block their view with my body.

My heart drops when I see her tugging at the engagement ring I gave her.

I've reached down and grabbed her hands in mine before I can even think. I want my claim on her finger.

"They'll see it!" she hisses. "You'll be dealing with the fall-out for eternity!"

I pull her out of the car, slamming the door behind her and trapping her with my body and arms braced on either side of her on the metal. I lower my head to her ear. "Let me worry about that."

"I don't think I can do this," she whispers. "I'm not sophisticated and..."

I feel her shrug.

"You can, sunshine dragon. You can do anything."

That doesn't comfort her. She snorts.

"Do you trust me?" Because though I have my doubts as to the wisdom of this, the one thing I am certain about is that Ella is absolutely perfect for this situation and any other. She's smart and beautiful and capable.

"Yes." She doesn't hesitate on that point. My heart expands painfully.

"Then don't be nervous. Be my good girl, smile for the cameras, and stay by my side."

A tiny whimper escapes her.

"Can you do that for me?"

There's a beat where I'm convinced she's going to tear from my arms and flee, but she nods. "Yes."

"My best girl." I kiss the top of her head gently, and draw back.

Her chin comes up and I offer her my arm. She's a born queen, she just doesn't realise it yet. She rests her fingertips on my sleeve, delicate as a bird, the ring in plain sight as we walk past the paparazzi, flashes going off.

They usually irritate the fuck out of me, to the point I may have threatened to kill several of them if they turn up again. They continue to take the risk because this charity event is a who's who of London's mafia here, with not just my brother and me, but the kingpins of Westminster, Lambeth, and a dozen or so of the smaller mafias I'm allied with. But in this case, I don't mind them so much. I'll be proud to have photographs of me Ella on my arm and speculation that she's my girl.

"Mr Blackwood!" We're not more than two feet through the door before Tom, one of the students, rushes up to us. "That photo you liked? It looks sick blown up massive." He jerks his head and beckons us to follow him. "Come and see, Mr Blackwood."

Ella gives me a curious glance, and I clench my jaw as I guide her into the crowd, all of whom are watching us, and clamouring for my attention.

I nod, and manage with all the charm I'm known for. I.e. None.

This was a mistake. Every man in the room is eating Ella up with their eyes. I wouldn't be surprised if I had to beat off wandering hands. I've been seen at numerous prestigious events in London's social calendar, but I've never brought a date to this one, and everyone has noticed.

I scowl. I snarl. Possessiveness is in my every glance, telling them: Yes, she looks exactly the sort of woman you want to throw up her skirt and find paradise, but she's *mine*.

Ella is oblivious. Sweet girl.

"What is this event?" she whispers, looking around.

"A student art exhibition. And there's a charity auction of all the art on display, in aid of the school."

"How do you know about it?"

I shrug. "Just something I heard about."

The space between her eyebrows puckers, and though I can see this answer doesn't satisfy her, I'm not sure I'm willing to tell her the whole sad story of why I organise this. I don't want her pity.

Tom stands tall next to his photograph, and he's right. The black-and-white image of a derelict building reflected in a puddle is powerful.

"Well done," I say, and he glows.

"This is amazing, did you take that photograph?" Ella studies the photos.

"Yeah. You like it?" Tom's gaze flicks between the two of us, obviously conflicted as to whether he should talk to her. Natural instincts warring. Should he attempt to flirt with the gorgeous woman who is closer to his age than mine, or will self-preservation win out? Because I know I'm glowering.

"This is Ella, Tom. My fiancée." I can't help the possessive snarl I end on.

"Nice to meet you," Tom mutters, glancing at me warily. He doesn't know I'm a dangerous kingpin. All these kids are aware of is that I'm their exacting teacher for one afternoon a week.

I draw Ella closer to me. I did not think through how I would feel about anyone else looking at my girl, especially in that dress. Pride wars with jealousy—no—I'm not jealous, I'm *territorial*. She's mine—as we walk through the first room of artworks, the urge to show her off is stronger, but only just. I introduce her to each student as we look at their work, always as, *my fiancée, Ella*.

I keep my palm in the small of her back, or tuck her hand into the crook of my arm as I guide her through the art exhibition, and gradually, the need to keep her for myself gets under control and the enjoyment of showing her off wins out, even as people come to greet us with barely disguised interest in Ella. We look at a dozen pieces, the students eager to show me their portfolios. There's prestige in being the highest bid item at this event. It might be only for student work, but over the years I've ensured art scouts, and all sorts of influential people attend.

Ella catches sight of a painting on the other side of the room, and I can feel how she wants to go. But she stays glued to my side as I talk with a student. My good little assistant.

"Now, my fiancée is desperate to see our resident bookworm's piece," I say when the student—one of the less talented kids in all honesty, but I give her time and attention anyway—has finished gushing. "And since Ella is a fellow reader, I'm going to indulge her."

I look down at Ella, who blushes scarlet.

"What do you like to read?" the student asks Ella politely, and there's a beat of silence where I wonder what Ella is going to come up with.

"Science fiction. Mostly," she says faintly.

Sure. Is that what we're calling it now? What she was reading was definitely nothing less than pure girl porn. "Come on, let's take you to your home planet, *science fiction* fan."

Hiding my amusement, I lead her over to the picture that caught her interest, and Ella stands and stares at the canvas.

"I love it," she breathes. It's a clever painting that uses paper and paint to create a montage that looks different depending on the perspective. It's a hand stroking pages of a book, and there's light, yellow and cream and pink like a soft summer dawn that tints the edges peachy pink.

"I bet," I reply wryly. I'm not sure if I'm relieved or sorry that the girl who painted the image is temporarily not here beside it.

"What?" Ella's brow crinkles with confusion.

"What do you think it is?"

"It's a book," she says firmly.

I raise a sceptical eyebrow.

"Or a flower. Oh wait, maybe it's..." She sneaks a look up at me, and shyly looks away. "I don't know."

"Little liar," I murmur, leaning down to whisper into her ear. "You know what it is."

She blushes prettily and damn but I want to see that again and again. It is a book, but the placement of the book between a woman's thighs, and a man's fingers in the pages, gives it a very different vibe. Plus, there's a pink tint to it.

Flower? Sure.

I admit, I like this piece. It's utterly filthy in the most deniable way.

"Are you going to bid for it?"

"On an assistant's salary?" She shakes her head regretfully. "I don't have anywhere to hang it even if it was affordable."

She could hang it in my house if she moved in, if this was all real, and she was going to be my wife, rather than a fake because I took advantage of a compromising situation.

Fuck. First I all-but stalk her, parking outside her apartment building on the weekends and torturing myself with her being close and yet out of reach.

That probably counts as full stalking, actually. And half the time I give in and call, making up some crisis or other that I need her help with, just so I can spend a few hours breathing the same air as my innocent assistant. The woman I love more than anything.

"I could find you somewhere for it," I say eventually. "Maybe in the office."

And I recognise immediately it's the wrong thing to say, but I don't know why.

"That wouldn't be appropriate. Thanks though." Sometimes her eyes have gold flecks, streaks of fire for my sunshine dragon, but they're more brassy than flame right now. "I'm going to nip to the ladies, I'll be back." As she pulls away, I find I cannot let her go, my arm reaching to full stretch before I release her. She smiles, unsure, a touch sad, over her shoulder, blonde hair gleaming, the dress shimmering.

She's so beautiful in that dress. My heart aches. I should

have said I'd buy her a home to put the painting in. I'd buy her a thousand houses if it made her happy.

"Pretty bit of fluff you have there, big brother. Triplet swap?"

"Fuck off."

Severino, one of my identical brothers, sidles up next to me. "There are lots of pretty things to look at here."

Sev rakes his gaze over Ella's body and anger boils up my throat.

"I *don't* share."

He smirks, and doesn't comment that I might not share women, but I've been generous enough with other things over the years. "Oh, possessive about this one, are you? Interesting."

"No. Not interesting." Yes. I am possessive of Ella. What if she likes my more charming brother more than she likes me? What if he steals her away? I doubt he'd have any scruples about seducing an innocent like my sunshine dragon. She can't leave me. I'm not sure I could bear the dark without her.

I turn to Severino. My younger brother is dressed in a pale grey suit, and is smirking. After forty years, looking at Sev or Vito is still the same as looking in the mirror. Sev is slightly lighter. His temples are greyer than mine, his countenance not as gloomy. Vito is as dark as me, but more tanned.

Sev would probably try something with Ella only to piss me off. He does that as often as we help each other.

"Have you heard Vito is returning to London?" I change the subject.

"The only thing this city lacks is a *third* identical Blackwood." Sev rolls his eyes.

"Should we take over Mitchem and give it to Vito?" Sev

loves anything bloody and difficult, which what I'm suggesting would be. And is an excellent distraction from Ella.

"Sounds fun. But our third wheel hasn't accepted any gifts from us or anyone else, since he was eleven." Sev shrugs. "I don't think he'd appreciate it, and you already know that. So what I'd like to discuss is that bit of skirt you haven't stopped staring after. Have you told her the sob story of how you clawed your way out of poverty by—"

"Enough," I growl. "Leave her alone. I'll skin you alive if you touch her. No subtle drowning in a river for you. I didn't make a fuss about the spy you sent to be my assistant, Sev, just dealt with him. But she's *different*."

Cocky bastard nods with a smug, knowing look.

Then his head turns, and his whole demeanour transforms as he yanks his phone from his pocket and opens it up. A soft expression of longing crosses his face as he looks.

And I'm way too curious.

I snatch the phone out of his hand and see a grainy black-and-white image of a young woman. Sev has snarled and grabbed the phone back before I can take a good look, but I've seen enough.

"Your girl, Sev?" I tease.

He's silent, jaw clenched as he takes one further glance then tucks his phone into his inner breast pocket. Next to his heart.

"She's not..." And there's a flash of vulnerability in my brother's eyes that I haven't seen for years.

We regard each other, our usual animosity and competitive spirit giving way to our bone-deep similarities. He's still my brother. I might kill his spies, but anyone who tried to hurt him would regret it.

Unless it was Ella. I'd choose her over Sev as easily as breathing.

And I'd fucking liquidise everyone who dared touch her.

"Who is she?"

"I can't tell you. And it can't go anywhere. Just she's..." He shakes his head as he searches for the right word. "Precious."

I sigh. Well, I know about that.

"I'll keep your secrets, and watch your back, Sev. Haven't I always?"

And quick as a rattlesnake, he's back to his old self, snorting with derision. "Watch my back? As though I need you. I've saved you more times than you've saved me."

Actually, I've been keeping count, and I've yanked him back from disaster more often. But that's hardly the point right now.

"Go away before Ella sees you," I snap. I'm camping out until my girl returns. I haven't stalked her just to have to turn my fucking brother into a smoothie for touching her.

5

ELLA

When I look in the mirror to give myself a pep talk, I find it's hardly necessary. My cheeks are flushed, my eyes bright.

He *touched* me. Hasn't stopped touching me since we arrived, in fact. Sure, I know it's because we're pretending, but he's not really a cuddly sort of person. He's gorgeous in a remote, godlike way. I wouldn't have been surprised if he had kept a controlled three inches of space between us at all times, but no. It's as though he's convinced no one will believe we're a couple unless there are signs the size of roadside billboards that we're together.

I'm going to struggle to give that ring back. It's gorgeous. Exactly the sort of thing I'd have chosen myself. What will be almost impossible is returning to being his professional secretary tomorrow morning. How can I survive without his hands on me?

Without him praising me and keeping me close like he has tonight, it'll be January all year round.

Good to know I have imminent heartbreak and a lifetime of remembering what I'm missing out on as the price for this one evening of bliss. *Ten out of ten, Ella, great survival instincts.* I should have accepted being sacked.

But I can't regret it. I crave this insight into my boss. This event too, isn't what I imagined Mr Blackwood being involved with. There are well-dressed people, yes, but he's hardly talking to them, because every student wants to have his attention on their work, thirsty for his quiet nod of approval.

Which is definitely something I can empathise with.

Good girl. His words from earlier echo through me and I press my lips together. I can't allow myself to put any significance on the fact that I've never heard him say that to anyone else. But when he introduced me as his fiancée, his voice was deep and resonant like he meant it. And the protective sweep of his arm around me? The way he ensured I was included in each conversation, and always at his side. Umph. I'm going to be remembering this evening until I'm a hundred years old.

This is a fake date, I remind my perky, optimistic reflection. I am not his real fiancée, I am doing him a favour so he didn't make me unemployed after I was utterly inappropriate in his office.

Twice.

That second time? Oof. I guess the sun would be hotter than Mr Blackwood watching me touch myself, but not much else. Him touching me, obviously.

Good, now I'm even more flushed. Exactly what I needed.

Fake date, I remind myself, and, swallowing hard, walk back out into the intimidatingly large and glamorous hotel. There are so many well-dressed people, and it's crowded, all gold doors and glass everything and high ceilings. I try to return to the room with the artworks, but as I take wrong turn after wrong turn, panic sets into my tummy. I'm so out of my element here. My mother would say I have ambitions above my station in life, and I guess she's right.

I have to get back to Mr Blackwood.

To my boss. To Rafe.

Then, finally, I glimpse a painting and make for it.

I hesitate in the doorway. I half expected Mr Blackwood to be waiting nearby, and my heart sinks a little that he isn't. Look, it's logical. He's an important person, he can't be hanging around for his secretary, even if I am supposed to be his fiancée tonight.

Then I see him, then blink and do a double take.

Rafe was in a perfectly tailored dinner jacket earlier, complete with bowtie and fine white shirt. And now, he's wearing a different suit. Less formal. His hair is mussed, there's more stubble on his jawline, and while the black-tie attire is similar, it fits him differently.

I think it's him, but Rafe smiles at me when our eyes meet, which is weird enough, but everything in me is screaming that something is wrong. I'm so disorientated from getting lost, I think I'm dizzy. But then, I'm sure I don't recognise the pictures around me from earlier.

Gah, I'm an idiot. Maybe I drank more champagne than I thought? I'm imagining things.

He looks me up and down as I approach.

"Hey. Sorry, Mr Blackwood. I lost you. I thought you were wearing..." I stop myself before I say something intolerably stupid. "Not doing great today at knowing where you are." I give a little fake laugh.

"This might be different attire to what you were expecting from me," he replies smoothly. "Don't worry."

"Was everything okay while I was gone?" I'm suddenly aware that I have one job this evening: to be his fake date in order to run interference with anyone who wants to get a bit of him. And while I'm now uncomfortable with his presence, I still want my job. Both the fake one and the day job.

"Nothing was okay until you arrived," he says. "I'm very glad you're here. I'd like us to know each other."

But unlike how Rafe this evening has been constantly touching me, now he keeps his distance.

Whoever this is, it's not Rafe. There are three things that make me certain. My boss doesn't feel like that, and would never say it. Then there's the darkness in this man's eyes, a cold that I've never seen in Rafe's. But moreover, I'm not attracted to him.

Where Rafe sets me aflame with a single look, this man leaves me as unaffected as a fish in a flood. It's as though all the magic of him has seeped out.

"No." Am I losing my mind? But his hair is slightly different too, more silver than chestnut brown. I've watched my boss for months now. Studied him. I'm a connoisseur of Mr Blackwood, and this isn't him. "You're not Rafe."

The man grins, wide and amused. "You're smart. See why my brother likes you. Not many people see the differences between us. I'm Severino. The good-looking and charismatic Blackwood triplet."

"Oh!" Relief and understanding cascades over me, along with spikes of shock. He has two identical brothers. He's never told me, but then, why would he? But at least that means I'm not hallucinating. "I'm Ella Button. Rafe's..." I was going to say assistant, but should I say date? Claiming I'm his fiancée to his brother seems presumptuous. *One night* fiancée.

My heart squeezes unhappily. This will all be over much too soon.

Severino doesn't seem bothered by my odd response, chuckling darkly, and shoving both hands in his pockets. "Rafe really didn't tell you about me or our other brother, Vito. Interesting. I wonder what else he hasn't told you."

I glance around in a panic, looking for Rafe. "I should get back…"

"Has he told you about why he's here?"

Despite the tone that tells me he's about to reveal something Rafe wouldn't want, I stop, unable to help myself. More information about my boss is catnip. I'm more likely to roll in whatever his brother has to say like a furry addict than say no.

"He hasn't, has he?" Severino smirks, and it's Rafe's face, but the expression is totally alien to me. "Nothing about growing up in one of the roughest parts of London, all the things he did to claw his way out of poverty. Nothing about nights we went hungry, or how he got that scar on his shoulder."

A scar? I guess he must have lots, given he runs a mafia. But I've never thought about his body except in terms of how beautiful it must be. Not the uglinesses.

"You haven't seen the scar, have you? Or the tattoos." Severino guesses correctly, and gives me an even more appraising look. "You are very young, maybe he didn't want to scare you."

"I'm not a child," I grind out.

"Does my brother know, I wonder? Since he obviously hasn't got naked with you."

I bite my lip. I wish I could make some smart response. Instead, I opt to pathetically ask for more details about my obsession while I can. "So you didn't grow up rich?"

"No." Severino's smile fades to a sombre expression that's much more familiar. "Every penny of all our fortunes is from work, clever investments, and ruthlessness."

"Self-made," I whisper, and I can't keep the admiration from my voice. It's one thing to be born into wealth. To build it from nothing is far more impressive. "I knew he was."

"And did you know that's why he runs this charity event?"

That jolts me.

"He does?" I didn't, but now Severino has said it, it makes perfect sense. Rafe has a core of integrity I admire, but it's not splashy. He doesn't talk about the nice things he does.

"With me." Severino nods with a cynical edge. "We've shared a lot, over the years..."

What? A strand of hair has come loose, and I nervously tuck it behind my ear. Severino's gaze goes straight to my hand, then stills like he's in shock.

"Fuck." He laughs disbelievingly, but there's a shadow of sadness in it too. Longing. "He didn't tell me that, or I wouldn't have tried to get myself murdered. Nice ring. Congratulations on your engagement, Miss Button. How long have you been together?"

I stutter, unprepared for such a question, and furious with myself. Why didn't I insist that Rafe and I discussed a story?

Because you were distracted by his eyes on you while you touched yourself, the dresses he bought, and the sheer intoxicating feeling of being with him.

Thank you, inner snark. That's true but not at all helpful right now.

My body tightens uncomfortably. I'm going to be found out. What can I say?

"A year and a half," Rafe's reply comes from behind me.

"That long." Severino looks over my shoulder, blue eyes flashing. "You've been keeping secrets..."

"I was waiting for you at the other door," Rafe says to me, brows low and dark, handing me back my champagne flute.

"Sorry. I took a wrong turn, and then..."

Rafe sighs and nods, pulling me to him. "You got conned. It's me that's sorry." He glares at his brother. "I should have warned you about this DNA-stealing second-class prick."

"Shared genetics, such a joy." Severino rolls his eyes.

"I told you to stay away from my fiancée, Sev," Rafe snaps.

"She approached me, big brother." Severino gives him an innocent smile. "And how could I resist the opportunity to get to know my new sister-in-law-in-waiting. A year and a half and you didn't tell me about her, Rafe."

"No."

My heart twinges. That one denial, and it feels sore, because of course he hasn't told him about me, because this is only for one night.

Severino is unperturbed by Rafe's brevity. "I was just telling Ella about how Vito, you, and I went to this shitty school as kids."

"It's not a shitty school," Rafe snarls, his fingers tightening on my waist.

"Anymore."

"I don't care what kind of school it was," I interrupt, since this scene is presumably for my benefit. "It's clearly doing much better for these kids now, and that's all that matters. I'm not bothered by what happened in the past." And then, I don't know where I get the courage to do this from, but I tilt my face up towards my boss' and smile with all the soft gooey feelings he creates in my tummy. "Only the future."

"What about your cute little tutoring side-gig—"

Severino is cut off by a middle-aged woman in a suit ringing a bell and announcing that dinner is ready to be served, so please would we all tear ourselves away from viewing the outstanding artistic talent of her students, and make our way to the ballroom. She catches Rafe's eye and smiles as she disappears, and a lightning rod of jealousy crackles down my spine.

Severino nods and strides off ahead of everyone who funnels through into the next room.

"Who's she?" I ask as we join the line of exceptionally well-dressed people plus nervously excited students and their parents. I am trying to be casual and missing the mark by quite a way if my boss' speculative look is any indication.

"That's the art teacher," Rafe replies.

"So..." I've been absolutely curious about this for a year and a half. "Is this anything to do with Wednesday afternoons?"

Rafe's shoulders stiffen and his jaw goes taut, all the humour bleeding out of him.

"Come on, you can tell your fiancée." I aim for light-hearted.

"Yes," he says tightly.

"Your brother mentioned your tutoring, and all the kids seem to know you..."

It's like getting blood from a stone. Rafe nods.

"Are you embarrassed by them? Their art is amaze—"

"No." His head snaps around at that. "No," he repeats

more slowly. "I'm very proud of them. All of them." There's something tender in his expression, and while I might be making this up, I think there's longing. It's the same bleakness I see in him when he stares out of the window of his office.

"You like kids?"

He softens his voice. "I love kids."

"Do you want children of your own?" I'm pushing my luck, I know I am. Any moment Rafe is going to tell me to stop talking or I'll end up in a freezing river.

He looks at me curiously, that steel trap mind of his working. Then before I can react, he's grabbed my hand and pulled me to the side, out of the stream of people and into a secluded alcove screened by curtains. He crowds me against the wall, pressing his body to mine.

His huge, very male, very aroused body.

Cupping my jaw in both of his big hands, he gives me a scowl that says, don't scream.

My heart pounds. He's much larger than me. In this corner, mere feet from where people are filing past us to go for dinner, I'm at his mercy. He could snap my neck before I'd so much as cried out.

"I'd have a dozen." He scours my face with his eyes, but his touch is delicate, gentle, even as his expression is serious. "As many as my wife would allow."

I scoff. "For the practice?" My tone is light, but my question is sincere. Because only women with overactive ticking ovaries—I'm trying to tell mine that there's plenty of time, but they ache with wanting Rafe—and blue male aliens who are at risk of species extinction actually crave children. Human males just want sex, right? The instant gratification.

But as he has all of today, my boss surprises me. "Not

the practice, Miss Button. The act. Breeding." He strokes my hair and his gaze dips to my mouth, lingering. "Filling my wife up with seed until she's overflowing. Fucking her and making love, giving her orgasm after orgasm before I come inside her again."

His hands slide down to my neck, his thumbs stroking my skin, and apparently my neck is really sensitive. There's some sort of direct connection between where he's touching a relatively uninteresting place on my body, and the throbbing centre of me between my legs. With his words and that slow, deliberate caress, he's turning me on like I'm his to command. I'm wet. Soaked. Needy and hot.

"Yes, I want that," he says, voice husky. "Painting my wife's insides with reams of seed. Getting her bred."

I gasp, but he ignores me and continues.

"Making her come on my cock and telling her to milk out the seed to make a baby. Watching her get lush and rounded when she's pregnant. Caring for her while she's carrying my child, and protecting my family. I want kids with pretty, mixed-coloured eyes and quirky habits to teach about the world. To show art and business and how to survive. To support and cherish. You're correct that I want baby-making, Ella. That's part of it. I want the sex that means something and creates life. Sex that wrecks. I want *everything.*"

Oh god, I'm panting. I'm a girl-shaped puddle of desire and hormones.

"But right now, *you* need dinner. Keep your strength up." He pulls me out of the alcove, and I stumble after him into the ballroom filled with tables. He guides us to two empty places at a table near the front of the room. Pulling out a chair for me, he leans down, head level with mine, as I thank him breathlessly and sit.

I can't believe my stern boss just said all those things about sex and babies and *breeding*.

To *me*.

I'm reeling. In shock. It was so. Hot.

He whispers in my ear, lips brushing my hair, "*Everything*. Think about that, fiancée."

6

RAFE

Seeing *my* little assistant with Sev has done something to me. HR would have a fit if they knew I had pushed Ella—who is half my age—into a shadowed corner and whispered filthy words about breeding and fucking and covering her with my seed. Even with the deniability of saying, "my wife", there wasn't anything ambiguous about my hard-on.

Which still hasn't gone down as we eat dinner and make polite conversation. Our companions are Laurent mafia bosses Sebastian and Jeanette, of whom Jeanette is the most dangerous by a considerable margin, the Westminster kingpin, Benedict Crosse, and his sweet wife, and the school's head teacher, who is terrified of me. Without the teacher, I suppose it would disintegrate into mafia shoptalk, but instead we're all being civil.

After dinner the head teacher gets up and begins what I know from years of experience will be a long-winded speech about art (important), the impact of these charitable donations on the school (stupendous), and how humbled she is (blah). I might teach the kids, bid on the art, and ensure the biggest names of the respectable parts of the London mafia attend, but that doesn't mean I want to be bored to death. From Ella's glazed expression, she shares my opinion.

I grab her chair and yank it, including her, towards me. Ella lets out a muffled squeak but manages to give Crosse's wife a reassuring smile when she looks askance at us.

"Tell me about your book." With studied casualness I lay my arm behind her shoulders and turn to regard the stage, pretending to pay attention.

"What, *now*?"

"Yes. Now." Out of the corner of my eye I can see that her face is within kissing distance. It's so, so tempting. Would she let me?

"Aren't you supposed to be listening, given this is your charity?"

I shrug and I can't help but turn just enough to look at her lips. Plush. Dusky pink, the colour of old-fashioned roses. I'd like to press my mouth to hers and plunder her with my tongue.

"I..." Darting her head from right to left, she establishes that mostly people are listening to this interminable speech.

As I observe her, my imagination brings up the vision—so familiar from frustrated moments in the shower when I need relief—of her mouth around my cock. So damn pretty. But with it is the reason I've held back. She's too young for me, and too good and sweet. For all the sharp suits and legitimate businesses I hide behind now, I've done terrible things. She's an innocent princess, and I'm an upstart ogre.

But that doesn't mean I won't take advantage of our one evening together.

"Miss Button," I say sternly when she seems as though she's run out of courage, noticing a woman at the next table watching her. There are eyes on us. Of course, there are. It's part of being a London mafia boss.

"It's science fiction about alien males," she says, then winces and lowers her voice to a whisper as the woman eavesdropping raises her eyebrows. "They don't have enough..."

"What?"

"Look, it's about..." She casts around, and snags on the after-dinner hot drinks in the centre. "Let's say that in this book, there are cafetieres of coffee."

"Right." This is unhinged. I have no idea where this is going, and I highly doubt she was reading about caffeinated beverages when I caught her with her fingers in her knickers, pleasuring herself.

I know people say they love coffee and are addicted to it, but there are kinks and then there are kinks.

"*Endangered* coffee cafetieres, because the *evil teapots* have *removed* all the way the coffee produces..."

This is making no sense, but I'm amused nonetheless. "Caffeine highs...?"

"Sort of. They need *cups*..." She presses her lips together. "To *pour* their milk into, and then that will make..."

And suddenly, it's all clear. I think I'm beginning to understand. "Spoons."

"Yes, to make little spoons. And the teapots want the cups too, to pour their milk into, and make their spoons. But the cup in the story doesn't want to be used by the teapots, she loves the coffee."

I manage not to snort with laughter. Holding up the teaspoon from my cup of coffee, I add, "One might almost say, *baby* spoons."

Ella blushes.

"Baby spoons," she repeats, her lips twitching with mirth.

Blood surges to my cock. She was reading about baby making, was she? My girl was reading breeding erotica.

Maybe, just maybe, I wasn't imagining her response to me when I told her my fantasies earlier. A single glass of champagne had given me the excuse to say what's been in my heart all along: I want Ella to be my wife and bear my children.

The head teacher concludes her tedious monologue, and everyone claps. I don't. I'm not moving my arm from its place around my girl's shoulders for something as trivial as the teacher's pride. I've sponsored this event and am about to make an exceptionally large donation. That is enough. Raising my champagne glass is plenty.

"And does the coffee win his cup's affection?" I ask Ella under the cover of applause.

"Yep, they're on the run from the tea, and he rescues the cup," she replies, clapping enthusiastically for something I don't think she heard any more than I did. "And they're sheltered under a... Tablecloth, shall we say?"

"Are they indeed? And what happens after that?"

"The coffee..." She stops as the applause dies away and the first artwork is brought onto a hushed stage for auctioning.

"Tell me, Ella." I lean in and growl into her ear as the bidding starts.

"I didn't get very far after that. Reading, that is." She turns and our faces are close enough I can feel her breath on my skin. "Not to the coffee and milk *pouring*, I mean."

"But maybe there was honey involved. In the cup."

She nods and her mouth opens. Her pupils are big, pushing those pretty yellow and green irises to being pure gold.

"There's a cup full of honey, so sweet and ready for coffee, is that right?"

"Yes," she breathes.

"But maybe he touched the honey first?"

"He..."

And I know that she can't say this aloud, but for fuck's sake, what is the point of being a billionaire mafia boss if you cannot talk dirty in inappropriate places to the woman you love?

I push my fingers into her hair and hold her head in place as I murmur into her ear. "I bet he licked that honey. Honey and coffee—white coffee with milk—is the perfect combination for making babies. Did he lick up every drop of that delicious honey and cause an earthquake for his little cup? The one he was going to use to bring new life into the world."

She lets out a tiny noise.

Out of the corner of my eye I see a painting being brought onto the stage.

"The first item for auction," the head teacher chirps.

"We'll continue this conversation, later," I murmur to Ella. "We have a painting to win." And if I'm really lucky, my girl's heart.

7

ELLA

If you'd told me this morning I'd be turned on by my boss discussing hot beverages, I'd have... Alright, that figures. Everything Rafe does makes me burn with desire. But that conversation was like nothing I've ever experienced before with Rafe or anyone else.

Hilarious, embarrassing, sweet. The heated look in my boss' eyes when he realised what I was telling him. Ooof.

Even the embarrassment was delicious somehow, flitting over my skin and warming me from the inside out.

Then there was Mr Blackwood teasing me, playing with me. My serious boss made an actual *joke*. I think. A joke-like object, anyway.

I'm not sure whether the comment about a painting to win counts as a joke, because Mr Blackwood relaxes back into his chair, arm still slung carelessly behind my shoulders as the painting I liked earlier is carried onto the stage.

"Are you going to bid?" Rafe asks.

I shake my head. "I don't think so."

But I'm tempted. That painting of the book? I would love to own it.

"Shall we start the bidding?"

"One thousand." Rafe's voice, but with a cynical twist, comes from the other side of the room. It takes me a second to realise that it's not my boss miraculously being in two places at once, but from Sev, who's even more dangerous and more complex than he is.

My heart stops. Despite what I said, I was kinda hoping that the bidding would stay low, and I'd have a chance. A hundred pounds or something. Get it for one day when I have a closet-sized space of my own in London and it can take up the whole of a wall. I'd hang it over the window, would save on curtains. But yikes. Apparently, charity art by teenagers is as outside of my budget as housing is.

"Want to bid for me?" Rafe says, and smiles when I snap my head around in disbelief.

"How would I know when to stop?" A thousand pounds is a lot of money.

"Here." He takes my hand in his, wrapping his fingers over mine. "I'll let you go when the price gets too high."

"A generous opening bid," the art teacher is saying. "Anyone else?"

"Say ten thousand," Rafe murmurs.

"I can't bid that much! That's madness. You don't even want it!" It's me who likes this painting, not him.

"I'll find a place for it."

"Two thousand," says another voice.

"Three."

The price is getting crazy before I've bid, and continues in the background.

Rafe's hand is warm and comforting, and for a second, I let myself dream that this isn't a lie. Maybe he cares for me, and we're here because that's what we do. As a couple, we hold hands, and buy art, and spend evenings together. Tell silly jokes and make babies.

And suddenly I want that painting so badly my chest aches. Even if it ends up in some random corner of the office, I could visit it, right? I could look at it and remember how for one evening, I was Mr Blackwood's fake fiancée and basked in the glow of his pretend love.

"Nine thousand," Severino says, and the other person doesn't reply. There's a gasp, and I cannot allow Rafe's mean brother to have my painting.

"Ten!" I squeak. That's the number Rafe told me to bid, and it's out of my mouth before I can think through how stupid I sound.

Rafe tightens his hold on my hand.

"Twenty." Severino drawls, sounding somewhere between bored and irritated.

There's a gasp from the crowd, followed by a buzz of gossipy excitement.

O. M. G.

Twenty thousand pounds. That is a lot of money.

"Twenty-five." I feel Rafe's voice more than hear it, a soft command for my ears only. It sends a thrill skittering down my spine. He's still holding my hand, gripping it. I couldn't draw back even if I wanted to.

"Twenty-five," I repeat. I'm having an out-of-body experience. Bidding Twenty-five thousand pounds for a painting. A painting!

I thought Rafe would look over at his brother while they engaged in whatever brotherly competition this is, but when I peek up at him, I find his chin tilted down and his gaze on me, not angry, but soft. And I'm lost. I'm flying through the summer sky that is his blue eyes. They are the most beautiful natural wonder.

Forget the northern lights, rainforests, monarch butterflies, polar bears, and the ocean. They have nothing on Rafe's eyes. I'd trek around the world for the joy of seeing him.

"Thirty."

"Thirty-five," I reply.

As Severino keeps bidding higher, faster, Rafe's expression darkens with impatience, and my heart beats quicker as he nods and doesn't let go of my hand as I say the words that try to get him the painting.

"One hundred," Severino announces, and the round number sends another shocked gasp around the room. This is, after all, a charity auction for a school.

"You've proved your point, Sev," Rafe growls. "She bids a hundred and fifty thousand."

Severino barks out a laugh and gives an ironic bow. "I'll hold you to your promise, big brother."

"Sold!" The teacher is gleeful, and, I think, a bit dazed.

I'm in shock. What happened?

"Good girl." Rafe drops a brief kiss to my forehead then rises. In a few steps he's at the stage. My boss grabs the painting from the assistants, who give it up without a fight, and everyone looks on, scandalised, as he strides back to me and props the picture against his chair, facing me.

"For you. My future wife."

I could cry with how much I wish that was true.

Then Rafe yanks me up into his arms, hard against his big chest. His mouth finds mine, confident and firm.

A kiss.

Our first kiss. The first real kiss I've had, and yet it doesn't feel like a first. Rafe is utterly commanding, leading me with his lips and as my mouth opens, his tongue slips in, conquering, possessive. There's no hesitation, like we've kissed in this way a hundred times before. It's all just the caress of his tongue and the pressure of his lips sending sparkling pleasure to my core.

I'm dimly aware there is an audience, but the world feels irrelevant compared to the solid, heated body of Rafe.

I dig my fingers into his shoulders, and grip so as not to fall.

I'm so greedy for this kiss. It's hot and intimate, and like nothing I've ever felt. I thought his eyes on me were intense earlier? This is more.

His hands hold me tight at my waist and at my neck, under my hair. We're close, but I cram myself towards him anyway. I need more of him. When I touch my tongue to his he rumbles a groan in response.

My boss.

Oh my god I'm kissing my boss, clinging to him. This is all my office daydreams and secret night-time fantasies come to life. This might be a fake, but he's kissing me like he means it. As though I'm precious and beloved.

And it's possessive as hell.

Somewhere in the distance, there are whoops and cheers, along with a smattering of applause and some awkward British titters. I barely notice. Rafe strokes my neck with his thumb, still holding me as though he needs to check I'm real and touch me more, but can't risk letting me go even an eighth of an inch. He's hard all over and it makes me go molten. I'm as liquid as he is hot stone.

"And that, ladies and gentlemen, is my brother in love," drawls a familiar dry voice.

I'm dazed as Rafe gently releases me with one last firm press, everywhere.

The whole thing can't have been more than ten seconds

and yet my world is upside down. Because they're right. This isn't a crush. It's love.

I'm in love with Rafe Blackwood. The knowledge shoots through my arteries, making my blood sing as I stare up into my boss' serious expression. I knew I adored and admired him, but I'm such a goner. I'm so far gone into love with him I'm lost in space without even the stars to navigate by, and that kiss just showed me, revealing how lightyears from my past I am. I couldn't find my way back to an earth where I don't love Rafe in a million years.

Sliding his hand from my neck down over my shoulder and to my waist, Rafe flicks his blue gaze to the side for a second. As he returns his attention to me, I can't help but check what he was looking at.

Identical blue eyes stare back at me as I glance over. Severino.

Oh. Right. Maybe that was all this was, proving a point to his brother.

In love?

What did Severino say? *In love.*

Oh triple yikes, Rafe is going to be mad at his brother for that.

"A very generous engagement gift, Mr Blackwood." The head teacher's excited voice interrupts my thoughts. "Very generous. Thank you so much. I'm sure you'll be very happy." She babbles on.

With an impatient snap of his eyes, Rafe lifts the massive canvas from where he leaned it against his chair and sort of slings it over his shoulder.

"Come on." He grabs my hand, and everyone is staring, with some amused looks and some scandalised, as he drags his new painting and his fiancée away, both possessions equally helpless to resist.

"Thank you!" the head teacher calls. "Shall we move onto our next lot? This is work by—"

"Ten thousand," Severino says loudly. "Can't have my brother steal all the good shit this evening."

As the delighted crowd gasps, I glance back. Severino gives me a friendly wink before Rafe pulls me out of the door.

Outside the hotel, the winter night air bites at my bare arms.

Rafe leans in and his warm breath tickles the little hairs next to my ear and sends a frisson of awareness down my spine as we walk out. There, waiting as though they knew, is Rafe's limo.

And that's it. Our agreement is all but over.

I'm sick with the inevitability of it. I'm not ready and I don't want this to end.

One evening as his fake fiancée to keep my job, that was the deal. And with heart-wrenching abruptness it's finished. I wish we could have danced until dawn. Until midnight at the very least, but no. It's not even that late and I guess Rafe didn't enjoy himself since he's put a stop to it so early.

If I begged and cried and stamped my feet like a toddler, would he reconsider? Would he return to the party and be my fiancé for one more hour? I'm addicted already. Mr Blackwood as my boss is hot, but as my future-husband, luring me in with little touches and sweet gestures?

Disaster.

Rafe seriously expects me to go back to calling him Mr Blackwood and organising his diary, and never think of the night that he laughed with me, and whispered flirty, filthy words in my ear about breeding, gave me champagne and a beautiful dress and made me feel like I was his singular, special fiancée rather than his little virgin assistant.

This is impossible. I can never go back. I'm ruined for life and if I have to be just his secretary again, I'd rather eat ice cream and cry on my own for the rest of my life than face Mr Blackwood being harsh to me every day and remember the one night when he said I was lovely.

So when he opens the door to the sleek black limousine for me, I stop and shake my head.

"I resign."

8

RAFE

Up until this moment, I wasn't sure. I thought perhaps this evening could be enough for me, that I could end it and accept Ella was only mine for a night.

Nope.

She's mine from now until eternity.

"You're not resigning."

"Yes, I am." She shivers in the cold, and I'm not thinking straight as I strip off my dinner jacket. I should just bundle her into the car, but instead I nod to my man to pick up the enormous canvas and remain here in the crisp, chilly London night air, pretending that Ella has a choice.

She grumbles like a disgruntled kitten as I cover her.

"I can't take this."

"Yes, you can. And you're not resigning," I say more gently, running my hands over her shoulders in the oversized coat.

She tears herself away from me, crossing her arms. But I notice she snuggles into the warmth of my jacket.

"I don't understand. Why do you want me to remain as your secretary?" she demands. "You're always so critical. Some days, it's just my mother all over again. I only want to make you happy, and you find fault with my work."

I'm rocked back on my heels. She doesn't know that she makes me happy? "Ella."

"No." She turns away.

"Ella, look at me." I make my voice unyielding. Like the times when I couldn't bear to spend an evening without her, so I made her redo work that was entirely perfect, just to have the excuse to put off her leaving.

She pouts but obeys.

"Such a needy little thing you are, my lovely girl." I take her chin between my thumb and forefinger. "I didn't realise you felt unappreciated. That ends now."

She blinks up at me in disbelief.

"And I'm a selfish arsehole."

That elicits a snort and a nod.

"Forgive me. I thought you knew from the way I want you with me constantly, that it was never about the quality of your work. That you're everything to me. I find fault so you stay with me longer, and I can stave off the loneliness for another hour. And unlike your stupid parent, I would never let you go."

"Really?" she asks doubtfully. Her lovely blonde hair glints in the streetlights. She's practically a beacon herself, my sunshine dragon, even when she's dulled by worry.

"You're incredible. Beautiful. My perfect secretary," I purr. "The sexiest woman I've ever known and the sweetest."

"Oh." Her mouth drops open. Then she returns to her pinched sadness. "You're just saying that because you don't want me to quit."

"Nope." I grab her waist and pull her to me, hard. So

she can feel the full length of my erection pressing into that soft little belly of hers.

"I'm saying that because it's true and I need you to smile as you take the whole of my big cock like a good girl."

"Boss," she pleads, sounding heartbroken. "I can't do this. I quit."

Panic flares in my heart. I'm not losing her. Never. "I'm offering you another job then."

"I'm not going to take it."

"Wife."

"What?" Her eyes fly to mine, wide with surprise.

"Full pay. Benefits. Company car." Love. Obsession. Breeding. I don't mention those. I'm not sure it will help my case.

"But," she splutters, and her laugh is hollow, with a bit of a hiccup. "Eighteen months and you've never made a single joke, Mr Blackwood. Then one evening and you make two!"

"It was at least three, but this isn't a joke."

"Don't be mean," she whispers, and looks away.

I grab her neck and gently but firmly push her jaw with my thumb until her eyes meet mine again. "I'm not joking. I'm offering you a position."

"A job as your *fake* wife," she says so softly it's barely audible.

I don't need her to love me. I tell myself that, even as an ache in my gut reveals it as a lie.

"If that's what you want it to be. But this job would be a full-time, permanent role. Twenty-four hours a day."

"That's the point, Mr Blackwood. I can't..."

"Why not?" I demand. Anything. I'll fix it.

"I can't tell you."

She closes her eyes, so I lean down and place soft kisses

on her neck. She whimpers. My girl is so responsive for me. I'm certain she'll come so easily, just like when she was touching herself in my office. When I reach her ear I murmur, "Tell me. Whisper it, just like you told me about the book."

However she needs to say it.

"Don't make me," she begs, hiding her face in my shoulder even as her hand creeps up, brushing my neck before combing into my hair and holding me.

I brush my cheek on hers, then press a kiss to that smooth skin. "Generous salary, unreasonable boss, will require you to be on call seven days a week for adorable children, and a husband who wants to fuck you."

"An unreasonable husband and a boss who wants to fuck me?" She peeks up and a wistful smile creeps to the edge of her mouth. "This sounds like a lot to deal with."

"Then say yes."

"No."

I smooth my hands down the curves of her body, and although she's saying no, she's holding my hair so firmly I'm sure this isn't an issue that she doesn't want me. She's not letting go.

"Why not, Ella?"

There's a beat of silence and I think of all the reasons she could say. That I'm too old for her. That's the only one I can't resolve. Everything else is negotiable. Me being a mafia boss? Fine, I'll change my career. My grumpy personality? I'll smile if she's with me.

"Why can't you be my wife?"

"Because I love you."

It's electric.

I tug against her grip on my hair so I can see her face, ignoring the tear of pain because my heart is exploding with happiness, heady and sweet as spiced sugary alcohol, to every part of my body.

"Say it again," I order her.

Her hazel eyes meet mine and in the flecks of gold and green and grey, I read that, reluctant as she is, this is the truth.

"A year and a half, Rafe. I've wanted you for eighteen long months. I'm not going to torture myself—"

"Forty years. I've been waiting for you for forty years."

She blinks in confusion.

"I've been waiting to fall in love for my whole life. I never believed it would happen until you implanted yourself into my office as my assistant. And I've been stalking you since the beginning." Fuck it. If she loves me, I'm all in.

There's a suspicious expression on her face, but she still hasn't relinquished her grip on my hair.

"I thought so..." she whispers. "All those times you were waiting outside my building when you picked me up to work on the weekend."

"I couldn't stay away," I confess hoarsely. "Ever since I met you, I craved you."

"My boss..." There's wonder in her tone. "*My* boss."

"Possessive little sunshine dragon," I whisper. "I'm yours. I always was."

"I can't believe it. My gorgeous boss being in love with me isn't real. This is something that happens to heroines in books, not normal girls like me."

Well, if that's easier, I'll try that route to ensuring she understands. "I still didn't hear exactly about that book you were reading. How does it end?"

She groans. "It's so embarrassing."

"Perfect. Tell me." I like to see my girl blush.

"You'll think it's silly."

I push my hand into her hair, mirroring how she's holding me, and almost purr at how soft it is. Everything about her is made for me. Giving her my most serious look, I tell her, "I will never think anything about you or what you like is silly."

And I consider it a success that she doesn't hesitate this time. She does trust me, with this at least.

"It's a romance. It ends happily ever after."

"Would you like to do that?"

"Happily ever after?" A smile tugs at the corner of her mouth and begins to shine in her eyes. A dawning realisation that this is real.

"You and me," I confirm. "And there's breeding, isn't there? The coffee wanting to make little spoons with the cups."

"Yes," she says faintly.

"We could do that too." I hold my breath.

"You said earlier...?" She makes a strangled sound. "Do you really want all those things you said about breeding your wife? If that wife was me?"

"Short of putting my whole heart, bleeding and beating, into your hands, Ella, I don't know how to make it any clearer that I'm in this. A baby or twelve. A family. Us."

But there's still disbelief in her expression when I dip my head to look into her eyes.

"Okay, fine." I huff out a breath. "I'll say it. I don't care that I'm too old for you—"

"—You're not!" she protests.

I ignore her because I am, and we both know it.

"I want the whole thing, Ella. I want to fuck you sweet and hard and loving and rough. I want to pull your hair and slap your arse for being so delectably naughty. I want you by my side all night as well as in my office all day. I want to hear if you squeak when you come when you're on my cock, or if it's just when you're touching yourself.

"When you need help of any kind, when you're sad, or happy or excited, I want you to turn to me. I want to be the first person you think of when there's a crisis or a celebration.

"Ella, I have been in love with you since we met."

As I've said all this, realisation has dawned, sweet and light like a summer morning, on her face.

"You were so grumpy." But she's smiling and loops her hands around my neck. The movement pushes her breasts onto my chest, and I groan, even as my heart becomes an overfilled helium balloon. I might float away with happiness. I clutch at her.

"I couldn't be nice to you. There was keeping myself closed off, and there was fucking you over the desk as I repeat that you're *mine*. There's really no middle ground here."

I roll my hips and hell, but this is good. She is going to feel like heaven.

She squirms against me. "I'll take the second one."

"Being mine."

"I always was," she admits sheepishly. "I've been head over heels for you from the first day."

"Have you indeed?" I grin. The first full, genuine smile I think I've had for years. "Then I'd better get my future wife home and work on breeding her."

9

RAFE

I ditch the painting next to the front door and tumble a giggling Ella—that's the best sound in the world—into my arms.

"Rafe!" She hooks her hands at the back of my neck as I carry her bridal style through my house and kick open the door to my bedroom.

"I'm not delaying anymore, Ella." I toss her onto the bed and the breath is bounced out of her. "There has been far too much restraint."

No waiting, I'm on her, braced over her, shoving my knee between hers to push her legs apart and getting my lips to hers in a filthy kiss that's a prelude to the way I'm going to lick and fuck her.

"There's something I have to tell you," she pants out when I drag my mouth down to kiss her clavicle.

"Is it how you'd like me to give you a baby?"

She lets out a little cry and squirms.

"Or how you can't wait to feel me filling you up, right to the brim? First with my cock, then with so much come it'll seep out of you for days."

"Yes, I want that. Yes."

"Good. Because I don't think you could stop me doing it now. You love me. I love you. And I bet you're soaking wet for me, just like you were—"

"I'm a virgin!"

That stops me. I raise my head.

She's never had sex with a man?

"Rafe, you're grinning!" She gives me a playful slap on the chest.

I am. I'm delighted. I get to introduce my girl to all the pleasures of lovemaking.

"Was this really what I had to do to make you smile?" she adds.

"Yep." I return to kissing her, nuzzling her neck. "Should have been your opening statement."

"Hi, I'm your virgin assistant..."

I reach the neckline of her dress, and tug it down to get access to those tits I've been dreaming of since we met. I reveal one perfect soft berry-coloured nipple.

"Please bang me and, oh!"

One light pinch and she's gasping. Yeah, that's it. So sensitive, my girl. She's going to be perfectly responsive for me.

"Breed you," I finish for her, then get her nipple between my teeth and lick at the point. "Over and over until you're full and ripe."

She clutches at the back of my head. "You don't mind I've never done this before?"

My grin broadens. She's all mine, and she thinks I might be disappointed that my greedy self gets every part of her. Hardly. "I love you. I wouldn't mind anything you did."

She combs her fingers through my hair, and I didn't realise how much I longed for her touch. For a second I'm transfixed. It's different from what we've done today so far. Not for show, not for lust. It's pure affection.

"I love you too."

And I needed that as well. Can't wait to hear her scream her love as she comes time after time tonight, and all the nights hereafter.

"Rafe. Skin. I need to feel your skin." Then she's sliding my suit jacket from her shoulders and fumbling with my belt.

I'm far more interested in her body than doing more than simply releasing my cock, but Ella is focused, taking no notice as I grab handfuls of her dress and pull it up. I tug off my tie and finally touch her bare thighs. Oh god she's wearing stockings.

"Fuck, Ella, are you trying to kill me?" I groan as I squeeze her deliciously soft skin.

"Help me get this off," she demands, tugging at my shirt.

"Once I have you naked." A compromise.

A cute little growl—like a cross kitten—escapes her as she works on my shirt buttons. We're both all hands and impatience. "Rafe! I have to see you. All of you."

"I need you too much to wait—"

"Please"

"Yes. Yes." And because I'm gone for this woman, I obey. Plus, she's wise. We're going to do this right. With all the time and love in the world. Keeping one hand in her hair, I drag off the clothes that seemed a good idea earlier on in my life. Suave and sophisticated and the kind of thing that would impress Ella when actually every stitch is just a fucking inconvenience. I get off my shirt with a scatter of buttons that makes Ella gasp.

I think it's because of the way I've destroyed my clothing, but no. She's instantly distracted from undoing my trousers, running her hands over my exposed chest with something very like awe on her pretty face.

As I flick off my cufflinks and let the shirt drop, she trails her fingers over the tattoo on my chest. A gold, red, and orange dragon.

"A sunshine dragon," she breathes. I nod when she blinks up at me. "When did you have it done?"

My heart squeezes. When I was in the pits of despair. When I needed something that was vibrant and bright but also uncompromising in their ability to scorch me into continuing.

"Years ago. Before you were even born, my little sunshine dragon." I almost don't tell her the rest, but her presence is like a truth drug. I can no more lie by omission than I could cut my own heart out. "When I first needed something sunny to balance my darkness. But I knew you were meant for me when I first called you that. This," I indicate the tattoo, "was just a premonition. Because when my mind was falling into the black pit the second time, you were there."

We stare at each other for a long moment, and I think she maybe begins to understand the depths of how important she is to me. Because my sunshine dragon *smiles*.

"And this? She reaches for my shoulder where the scar left by the Camden mafia boss being unimpressed with my upstart, thieving ways is in evidence.

"I'll tell you the whole story, I promise," I reply. In as much gory detail as my bloodthirsty wife wants. "But right now, I want to focus on you, not what happened before."

"You swear?" But she's already pressing kisses to my shoulder rather than examining it.

"We have all the time in the world, sunshine dragon. I promise. I'm never letting you go."

"Good," she whispers, and slides her hands down my dragon tattoo to the scatter of hair that leads down and by my waist. She explores with a throaty sound of appreciation that sends even more blood pumping to that already rock-solid length.

She was so right. I need us both naked.

Clothes. Totally overrated now I've had Ella's touch on my skin. Her hands are unbelievably soft.

So the same goes for her dress as for my shirt. Five minutes ago, I'd have told you that dress was the most perfect foil for my future wife. Nope. It's a goddamned rag.

Which is why when I can't find a zip, I untangle my hand from her hair, grab both sides of the dress' neckline, and rip.

Ella is so involved with my tattoo, she only realises too late that I've destroyed her dress. She goes rigid with shock and I'm an animal, still holding the tattered silk in my hand, heart racing, cock harder than it has been in my life, staring lustfully at her naked tits, now bared to me.

"Rafe! That was expensive!" she scolds.

"I'll buy you another." I cup her breast, a perfect handful, and stroke the pert little nipple. "Plus, it wasn't. Not compared to how priceless the feel of your skin is."

"Who is this charmer—mmm." She moans as I roll her nipple. "And what have you done with my surly boss?"

"Now he has everything he's ever wanted, your boss isn't surly. He's happy."

"I'm happy too," she murmurs back as I tug at her lacy white knickers.

Good girl that she is, she lifts her hips for me, and they slide down her long legs. Then her pussy is exposed and just as mouth-watering as I anticipated. I strip off the rest of my clothes, never taking my eyes from the pink, wet prize I've unveiled, and she shrugs out of her ripped dress.

Then blood is pounding in my ears as finally—finally—I'm kneeling between her legs. Ready to worship my princess as she deserves.

I should start with tender kisses and gentle words, but she's made me crazy. I press my teeth into her supple thighs, one at a time and she moans. It's only by sheer will that I manage to tease her a bit, kissing at her thighs, getting closer to where she's pink and smooth. The scent of her cunt lures me in, sweet and heady. And fuck, she's so wet. I'm covered before I even begin, my mouth watering for the taste of her and my cheeks smeared with her desire.

The initial lick is the same relief and high as an ice cream on a summer day. Creamy and sweet and salt, and the way she moves beneath me, restless and needy, makes my cock ache.

There's time for that. I'm going to be balls deep in my girl when I first come tonight. Then hopefully many, many times again, this night and for the rest of our lives.

"Your honey is delicious," I murmur, then go back, urging her legs wider with my palms until she's totally bared to me, exposed but for my hungry mouth.

I go down on her like I'm starving. Which, basically, I am. There have been far too many years without her. In response, she whimpers and trembles. In the hierarchy of needs, it's now air, water, and feeling my girl come. Food? Pfft. Sleep? Who needs it? If I can just have Ella come on my fingers and my cock and my mouth three times a day, I'll be fully nourished. Watching will do, but I'm desperate to feel it on my tongue as she pulses with pleasure I gave her.

Releasing one of her thighs, I bring my hand to my lips and when I flick my gaze up to see my girl's expression, I find that while her eyes are hazy, she hasn't closed them. Nope, she's looking at me like she's fascinated, almost as obsessed as I am with her.

I raise my head and, with deliberate slowness, I slip my forefingers between my lips, as lewd and sensual as I can make it. Obviously, this is unnecessary. She's wet enough on her own, never mind with me having been licking her. But it's all part of me teaching her how much I enjoy her.

"Oh!" Her mouth falls open and her eyes go wide. "What are you doing?"

Unable to restrain my smile, I lower my hand to her soaking entrance. "Finger fucking you until you come."

"I thought we were..."

"We will," I assure her, pushing one fingertip in and she pants. "So tight. So hot. You're going to come on my fingers and tongue. I'll open you up a bit, because you're small, and I'm big." I'm easing a finger in and out of her, just up to the second knuckle. "And it's going to take you time to adjust. I'm going to finish licking you, so I feel that first sweet orgasm on my face. Then I will push my fat cock into you, stuffing you full."

Her eyes lose focus. I bring my finger out, then thrust two back in and she arches.

"I miss your taste," I say, and go headfirst back into licking her, chasing down her orgasm with determination. Before I was crazy but savouring her, now I'm animalistic. I plunge my fingers in and out, and my tongue is insistent.

"Rafe," she sobs, and begins to shake.

I don't answer. All my energy focuses on getting her off. I've never wanted anything so much.

She tenses and I note it, licking that exact spot, over and over. And I'm rewarded not only by the clench of her pussy, grabbing my fingers as I beckon her through the onslaught, but her scream.

Every shudder and involuntary jerk as she comes makes arousal and satisfaction spike in me in equal measure.

"That was so perfect," I say against her skin as I withdraw my touch to soft kisses over her inner thighs, allowing her respite. "The first is so sweet."

"First?" she replies vaguely. "There's..."

"More, yes. At least three, beautiful girl. We have time to make up for."

She gives a strangled laugh and relaxes into the bed. "Yes, boss."

Rising up, I leave her pussy with a pat of reassurance. *Don't worry, I'm coming back for you.* I slide next to her and pull her onto her side, raising my eyebrows. "You want me to still be your boss?"

"Maybe?" She licks her lips.

"You like me telling you what to do, huh?" A grin tugs at my mouth. "Did you enjoy reading in my office earlier when I instructed you to? Touching yourself the way I ordered?"

Cheeks pinkening, she nods.

"And at the party?" I ask with a flash of insight. "Did you like being on my arm, at my side? My good girl."

"That too. I liked feeling as though I was your... pet." She whispers the last word. "When you were showing me off."

"You are my pet. My cherished girl. My favourite. Now." I roll onto my back, taking her with me and the sound of her giggle fills my soul. "Time for you to give me that V-card."

10

ELLA

"What, from here?" I push myself up on his chest and look down at him doubtfully. He smiles back.

My. Boss. Smiles. At me. Blue eyes twinkling with mirth.

As his gaze flicks appreciatively down, I'm suddenly aware that the sturdy surface supporting all my not-inconsiderable weight is *him*. Beneath my palms, there is dark hair scattered over his pectorals, which are entirely solid and warm.

His whole body is a dream I never want to wake from. Don't ask me why that happy trail on his lower belly makes me like jelly, I don't exactly know. But he's beautiful. His arms are muscled, his shoulders broad. The sight of him coils arousal heat between my legs.

And that tattoo. The dragon curves around his side, wings open, bright and determined, black, red and gold, breathing fire. It speaks of his determination and the power he's built up from nothing.

"Yes," he replies finally. "From there, little sunshine dragon. You're going to do your job—which is to use your boss' cock to take your virginity. I'm going to instruct you and praise you and encourage you, as I should have done since day one."

"What, you should have laid down in the office eighteen months ago and had me straddle you?" I quip.

He grabs my hips and pushes me back so my pussy is right over the thick, hard ridge of his cock, then flexes upwards. The movement shoots pure bright pleasure through me, so quick I immediately want it back. Not an orgasm, just excitement, as though every cell in me is attuning itself to him.

"Yes. I should have. You were meant to be mine and I wasted a year and a half telling myself you were too young and innocent for a grumpy old bastard like me."

"I like your grumpy bastard side," I laugh. Easing down as though in a press-up, I kiss him lightly on the mouth. My breasts brush his chest. "And you're the perfect age to know things to teach me. To be powerful and strong and look after me as no one else ever has." Who needs family when I have him?

"I will look after you, in every way. Don't you worry." He runs his hands possessively down my sides, then up my spine until he reaches my hair, gathering it together. "So beautiful." I arch as he draws my head back, tugging on my hair the perfect amount to sensitise my scalp and send pleasure skittering through me, right to my core.

Rafe slowly pulls harder, and I gasp and scramble to lift myself up, holding myself on that delicious chest of his.

"Sit on my cock, pretty girl," he says in a deep rasping voice that makes me tremble. "Then I want you to come all over me before I flip you over and pound you into the mattress. Fill you up and give you a baby."

I shudder with the electric heat from his words. Dirty.

I'm so glad I got him naked, but if I thought it would make him less intimidating, I was dead wrong. His self-assurance is bone-deep, not some flimsy thing that relies on his perfectly tailored suit, or even his wealth and power.

"Now, Ella. I can't hold back much longer," he warns. Releasing my hair, he smooths his palms down my front, pausing to stroke my nipples and squeeze my waist, until he reaches my thighs. "Push yourself up, and give yourself to me."

My muscles tighten, and before I know it, he's reached behind me to wedge his cock into place, right in the soaking folds of my sex.

"That's it," he croons. "Feel how hard I am for you, my love. I want your snug little pussy, and I can feel how desperate you are for my cock."

My legs, not used to this position, are already struggling.

"Just sit down."

But... He's so big at my entrance. I don't know if I can do this without breaking in two. I wobble uncertainly.

"Ella," Rafe rumbles. "You're going to take my cock tonight. I know you can, I know you will."

I nod, because I really do want to. It's just...

"I'm afraid."

"I know." He touches his fingertips to my chin and draws me to look into his piercing blue eyes. I'm immediately lost. "But you're my brave girl and I promise this is going to feel like heaven once we get past breaking you in."

"Oh god, why is that hot?"

He chuckles as he brings his hand to my clit and begins to circle his thumb.

"It will feel superb for me from the first. It already does for me. The soft folds of your pussy on the tip is enough to drive me wild. But you told me you didn't think I appreciated you. So look at me and see the truth, my love."

It's like that touch is a release catch, and I begin to sink onto him. And yeah, ouch. It's a pinch that spikes me, but it's also a delicious stretch.

"See how much pleasure you're giving me," he continues without hesitation, and yeah, I can see. It's obvious he's enjoying this. "Let me tell you that your tight pussy is the best thing I've ever known. That I love you and I'm going to make up every bit of pain to you a thousand-fold in pleasure like you've never known as I lick you and fuck you and make you come and tell you that you're the best thing that's ever happened to me."

I sink down just enough that the head of his cock goes in. I pause, keening from the back of my throat.

"My good girl. I'm resisting the urge to thrust upwards and fill you completely," he says through gritted teeth. "Because you're doing a great job. I'm proud of you."

I wiggle my hips, and get him in a bit more. It's so tight. He's hard and hot and I can feel this is only the start. I'm about to say I can't do this when my body relaxes, gives, and I slide right down, our hips touching. I swear I go cross-eyed. It's like nothing I've ever experienced before.

"That's it." Rafe strokes my clit, and where I was full before, stuffed, now I'm on the edge of something wider and more overwhelming. Pleasure. "You're doing so well."

He's taken what I said to heart and is making sure I can't doubt that he thinks I'm doing well. As I ease myself up and down on his cock, he caresses my body appreciatively, that hooded gaze eating me up.

"You're too big," I complain, and the bastard laughs.

"You'll learn to like that," he says, with a smug smile,

remaining still beneath me but stroking my body as though familiarising himself with every part.

Experimentally, I move, lifting myself up and down on top of him. The twinge of pain recedes every time I hit the bottom. The tip of his cock feels as far into me as my throat. He's taking up all my inside space, reforming me around him.

And damn, but I like it. I'm gaining confidence as Rafe whispers sweet nonsense words, repeating in a dozen different ways that I'm his and he's pleased with me. And all the time, the movement of his thumb on my clit is spiralling me higher.

Then my boss is sitting up, his other hand is on my hip, gripping me, encouragement and insistence that I take him, deeper, faster.

I bring my hands to his shoulders to steady myself as I do as he tells me, my thighs burning with the effort. But it feels good, so good, looking into my fiancé's eyes as I take his big cock into me over and over. I tighten my grip as pleasure closes on me, and Rafe coughs.

"Fuck, Ella," he rasps.

For a second, I don't know why.

Then humiliation and horror pours over me as I realise my hands have crept to his neck and... Oh god save me, I've been choking a mafia boss as I fuck him. What is he going to do to me?

I snatch my hands away, and try to draw back. But Rafe is quicker, grabbing my wrist and my hip, even as I wriggle.

"That's alright, sunshine dragon." He brings my palm to his neck, and wraps my fingers around as far as they'll go. Honestly, not very far, since he's so much bigger than me.

I'm frozen with disbelief and fascination—and I admit, a twinge of arousal—as he smiles, slow and dangerous.

"I liked it." He tilts his chin back, arrogantly baring his throat. "I said use me, ride me. Choke me as you take your pleasure, little sunshine dragon. I know you're wild as well as beautiful. I'm not afraid."

Tentatively, I nod, and lift up, the friction making me gasp. He grins, smug and in control even as I have my fingers over his windpipe.

"Fuck me like you mean it," he growls, and his hands return to my clit and my waist, lifting me up before ramming me back down onto his cock.

So I do. I push up and down, faster, my eyes crossing with ecstasy.

"Rafe." I say his name and it's a prayer to him.

"Take more." He flexes beneath me, thrusting up so my thighs slap onto his hips. "Tighten your hand."

I do, just a little bit, and his blue eyes glitter as he almost purrs.

"Rafe." I love the feel of his strong, muscled neck under my fingers. This powerful man, encouraging me, loving me. Spearing me with his massive cock.

"Pinch your nipples," he instructs.

I grasp for my breast, and I can't look away from his blue eyes. Then the shock of my own tweak proves him right to demand this. The almost harsh touch spikes right down to my clit, amplifying the pleasure he's giving me there.

The hint of pain is as good as the pleasure. It heightens every sense and suddenly, it creeps up on me, a wave that I swear originates with Rafe's ocean-blue, fathomless eyes. This orgasm is sharp and unexpected, and I dig my nails into his shoulders to hold on as it pulses from my clit outwards, making my whole body twitch.

Rafe groans and no wonder, because I'm strangling his

cock as I come, each wave softer but more intense, wrecking me. Eventually I give in, slumping down onto the sturdy, comforting warmth of my lover's chest. He's still inside me, incredibly hard, but I'm ruined. A destroyed girl. Broken. And Rafe has moved his hand from my clit, knowing somehow the exact right moment to stop.

He wraps his arms around me, and I vaguely register that he's murmuring praise. That I did well. That I'm his best girl, his sunshine dragon, and that he loves me. That I feel amazing around and over him and I'm the best girl blanket in the world.

I'm so satisfied, I'm melted butter.

Then without warning, Rafe's grip tightens and in an eye-blink I'm on my back, the air knocked out of my lungs, staring up at a darkly determined man over me.

"Two down," he whispers, then kisses me, hard. "Two to go."

O. M. G.

What have I got myself into?

11

RAFE

Much as I enjoyed having my girl on top of me, I'm obsessed with having her beneath me. I kiss her as I begin to thrust, gently at first, a smooth glide of my body into hers.

She's just as perfect for me as I imagined all those nights alone when I jerked off to the memory of the smile, the curl of her blonde hair around her shoulders, or the mornings when I took the edge of my need for her by a quick release in the shower fantasising about how her tits might look.

What I never thought about was how soaked and ready for me she'd be, and how easily she'd come when I touched her. I had no idea my girl wanted me and was so responsive.

Right now though, she's bathed in post-orgasm relaxation, completely pliable to my will, kissing me back and exploring my shoulders. I've never felt this close to anyone in my life. I want to smoosh her to me. I'd unzip my skin and keep her tucked to my bloody heart if I could.

"What about a bit more?" I reach down for first one thigh, then the other, and push them up, opening her for me to go deeper.

That gets her attention.

She lets out a cry of pure surprised arousal, and I kiss her neck with licks and bites and presses of my lips. The angle is different as I keep thrusting, taking my pleasure and giving to her too. I know it's hitting the right spot when she begins to sob and babble.

"I love you, what are you doing to me? I love you. You're so big—" She breaks off as I pick up my pace, driving into her harder.

"You're deliciously wet, the best thing I've ever felt."

She moans and writhes beneath me, then brings her hands down to my arse, digging her nails in, trying to get me deeper and faster.

For a moment I'm torn. The evidence that she wants me and needs more of my cock is gratifying. But at the same time, I'm hanging on by a thread here, and I promised her two more orgasms. If she urges me on like this, I'll spill inside her within minutes if not seconds.

"Uh-uh. You'll just take what you're given, Ella. Put your hands above your head."

Eyes wide, she obeys, and I grin, scraping over her body with my gaze, indulging in her nakedness.

"Good girl, well done. Keep them there." I slide my hand over her belly, relishing her soft skin and the way she's spread out for me, her curves on full show. "Your tits are amazing."

She gasps as I lean over and take one nipple in my mouth, kissing the plump flesh, then gently biting, and soothing the hurt with my tongue.

"Ohmygod, Rafe!" she cries out as I repeat the motion for her other nipple.

"That's it. Feels good, right?" I shift forwards and she opens for me, a perfect little flower that I'm defiling. My hips settle on hers, but I'm holding my weight off her as I bracket her head with my arms. Her hands creep to clutch at my hair and I growl.

"Hands above your head, Ella. I won't ask again, I'll tie you down."

"Yes, boss," she replies in a breathy whisper that goes right to the head of my cock.

And that title she gives me reminds me that as bad a man as I am, I've been a worse boss, and a tragically inept lover. She thought I didn't approve of her, didn't love her, and criticised her work.

I still have so much to make up for on that front.

Probably sex isn't the moment for it, but when were the two of us conventional?

"I always appreciated you, Ella," I whisper onto her skin between kisses. I keep her wrists pinned and move the other hand seamlessly between torturing each of her nipples in turn. "The coffee you brought me. The way you kept people from the office when I needed time to think. The way you listened whenever I needed to blow off steam.

"It's okay." Her voice is breathy. "What you're doing with your cock right now makes everything better."

"Don't tempt me," I chuckle despite myself. "Or you'll find every workday ends with me giving you an apology fuck."

She laughs, her throat vibrating where I'm kissing it, and that is the best noise in the world. Sweeter and more heart-warming than the sound of her coming. I'm going to do my utmost to ensure she laughs even more than she comes. Multiple orgasms and giggles for my girl.

If that means smutty books, oral sex constantly, and making love to her, who am I to complain? Hell, if it requires permanently hiring a stand-up comedian, I'd do it to hear my girl laugh.

"I am going to fuck you and compliment you as often as you need so you know you're loved and appreciated." I raise my head and look into her face. Her head is thrown back, she's breathing hard, and moving beneath me in time with my thrusts. "My clever girl, look how good at this you are. Figured out how to work with me to make it better for both of us. I love you so much. I will spoil you non-stop."

I reach up and stroke her hair and her flecked eyes gleam with gold.

"I'd like that." She's smiling.

"So will I, sweet one. I'm going to enjoy showing you how loved you are. Speaking of which, again," I demand. "Get there again for me, good girl."

"I can't, I can't."

"You can." My voice is stern, but the way she gasps makes me think that's alright. "Keep your hands there."

"I just need you to come too, Rafe, I want you to feel as good as you've made me."

"I will, I promise. After you've done your job, my love, and *come for me*." I don't mean to sound so commanding, but she doesn't seem to mind. I don't know how I'm lasting when she's all tight wet heat, soft skin, and she *loves* me.

With my fingers tangled in her hair, holding her head in place as I kiss her, I cram my hand between our bodies. We're both sheened with sweat from the exertion—and her from the orgasms—but I get to what I need. Her slippery folds, and the little nub hidden within.

Her response is gratifyingly swift. One stroke and she cries out, another and she's shaking, and then all I have to do is ease her through the climax and resist the way she's pulsing around my cock. I hold on, relishing her pleasure but keeping it separate to mine as I fuck her slowly, languid as a summer tide and tell her she's doing well. That she's my best girl, and I love her.

And this time, I think she believes it, body and soul. She watches me, eyes open as she comes, gloriously confident in revealing herself to me.

But unlike the last time, I'm not so patient. I've held out long enough.

"I'm naked, in you raw, sweetheart," I say, even as she's still fluttering with pleasure.

She lets out a moan that surges right to my cock. I can feel a release building at the base of my spine, threatening to tip over.

"Last chance before I make you pregnant and mine forever."

"I'm yours, I'm yours." She nods, eager, and every possessive instinct in me brightens at her words. "I want it all. Please."

12

ELLA

"That's it," he murmurs comfortingly as another wave of pleasure crashes over me. "So good. You did so well." He presses his mouth to my forehead in a tender kiss. "Just one more and then you're done."

WHAT?

"One more?" I squawk, finding my voice.

"Yes." My soothing lover is gone again, and my demanding boss has returned.

I missed him. I love both. His gentle side and his grumpy, abrupt side. Now that I know how to read him better, after he's let me in, I realise all the things that he did which showed his love. The way he wanted to be with me, talk with me.

"Rafe!" This is positive reinforcement gone mad.

"You want me to breed you." It's not quite a question from my boss. It's a growling demand for my surrender.

"Yes! I want you to breed me. Please. Fill me up. But I don't need to—"

"My sweet girl," he groans as he thrusts into me, fingers pinching into my hips. "I can't wait to see you have my child. Our child. One more, and I will breed you. Once you've come for me again."

The honesty between us is heady as the first sip of alcohol. I don't have to hide with Rafe, and finally, I understand him. Months of avoidance and concealing our feelings—our love—and now it's all bare. Our skin, yes, but the smile on his face lights his blue eyes in a way I couldn't have imagined. He's gorgeous. A bit bristly, grumpy, craggy, my beautiful silver fox.

The sensation of him inside me, fucking into me, is all-encompassing. I'm helpless, taking what he's giving, barely able to hold myself up and literally that's all I'm asking my four limbs to do right now, and that's way too much, apparently.

I shake and collapse as he makes me come again, the pleasure so overwhelming I can't think.

I had no idea sex would be like this, or that my body was even capable of these feelings.

And my heart.

Because as surely as he's invading my pussy and stretching me open for him, he's overtaking my heart with words of love and praise.

He's telling me filthy things about how wet and pink my cunt looks from this angle, and how I'm taking him so well.

Without warning, he pulls out, flips me over, and drags me up onto my hands and knees.

"What?" My head snaps to over my shoulder, where he's kneeling, a possessive look in his eyes and a promising smirk on his lips.

"I need you to come once more." The blunt head of his cock presses at my entrance. But unlike before, when getting his enormous length in was a struggle, I've adapted now. All I feel as he pulls me back onto him, like I'm his toy, is the most brain-melting stretch.

"Uhh..." I'm nonverbal. I can't come again, I'm sure about that, but I still want him in me for the amazing sparks and the sense of being his. Of being owned body and soul by my grumpy, handsome, billionaire mafia boss, boss.

I love him. It was always true, but the way he's putting me above everything else—first in his life and I've come three times already and he's not come once—proves I was right. I trusted him even when everyone else assumed he'd murder his next assistant. I saw past his bad temper. I helped get him the quiet he needed. This is my reward: his love, his lust, his attention to my body.

He slams into me from behind, over and over.

But it's not just for him. He must know what this is doing to me. My breasts are heavy and sensitive, hanging down. My clit is impossibly throbbing as he lazily circles over it. There's liquid evidence of my arousal everywhere. Drying on his cheeks, over my thighs, on his cock, dripping onto his fingers and soaking my folds.

The angle as he fucks into me from behind is unlike anything else.

"Come for me again."

I'm almost crying. Sobbing. It's too much.

"Ella," he says in that stern CEO voice that he's used with me over the last year and a half. "I said come for me. Come on my cock."

I can't. I'm wound so tight I can't even speak.

"I know you can, my beautiful, perfect girl."

Then, somehow, I'm close. I'm a touch away. The motion of his cock and his fingers keeps me on the edge.

"You won't get the seed you want until you come. One more, my come-slut fiancée."

That's it.

I break.

The bliss wracks me, over and over again as he continues thrusting and rubbing my clit. I'm still coming as he flips me, so I'm on my back. Then he slides into me, and his face contorts with pleasure. He trembles, but his eyes never leave mine as he thrusts, pounding me into the mattress until he stiffens and groans.

"Ella." He repeats my name as he fills me with wet heat, the pressure delicious, his come spilling out at the sides as he continues to pump.

It's magic. I've never felt this close to anyone. I'm bracketed by his arms, held, cherished. I couldn't imagine feeling this loved. It's like his love is buzzing in every cell of my body as he thrusts all the way home, as tight and hard and deep as possible and holds me there.

The sweat cools on our skin as we stay entwined, though he rolls us back over so I'm laid on top of him again. He covers my face with kisses and tells me that I'm such a good girl, that he's made me his, that I'm going to look gorgeous pregnant with his child. His cock remains inside me, softening only slightly, before hardening again.

"Rafe!" I can't believe it when he begins to push up into me. We're a sloppy mess, wet and a bit sticky, but he doesn't seem to care, so neither do I.

"You didn't think once would be enough, did you?"

I grip him with my inner muscles, and he growls. "Minx. I'm going to get you for that."

"Are you going to give me a baby, boss?"

His chuckle is strained. "I'm going to give you everything you ever dreamed of, and more."

"I'm too lucky," I gasp as his hand goes to my clit.

"Marry me."

"W-what?" My mind is blurry with the pleasure that's still echoing in my limbs.

"You heard. You have my ring on your finger, my seed in your womb. You're going to have my child. I think I've proved that I can fix that issue with my not telling you how much I appreciate you, and I promise you'll never feel overlooked again. You're the centre of my world, and I'm going to ensure you know that, every day." He reaches and strokes my cheek tenderly. "You have my love. Marry me and be my wife."

That was, I have to admit, a speech worthy of a sexy blue alien. And who could possibly refuse Rafe when his blue eyes are full of so much affection? Plus, he gave me four orgasms. So there's nothing else to say, but...

"Yes."

EPILOGUE
RAFE

6 years later

"Happy birthday, Daddy!" My eldest child and only son—so far—throws himself across the kitchen.

"Hey champ!" Turning and dropping the spatula I'm using to spread pancakes, my heart stops. "Watch the—!" I wince as Giovanni's head misses the sharp corner of the big oak table by a hair's breadth. Unconcerned, my son launches himself into my waiting arms.

I hoist him up and he grips onto me. Five years old, and a total cuddle monster, my boy. I know I'm supposed to be a tough mafia boss, etc. etc. But the uninhibited way my children love—they learned from their mother—puts a lump in my throat.

We've broken the cycle. Where Sev, Vito, and I are still prone to being wary and cynical, and more than a bit grumpy, all of our kids are full of zest for life. Safe. Cherished. Loved. They have all the support and care that we lacked.

"Daddy," Giovanni says into my shoulder. He's clinging on like a koala bear, so I go back to tending the pancakes, and he giggles. "Do we all have to eat pancakes because they're your favourite and it's your birthday?"

"It's Uncle Severino and Uncle Vito's birthdays, too," I point out.

"But they love pancakes even more than you do! Is that a being-identical thing?"

"You'll have to ask your sisters."

"Is what an identical thing?" Sev asks as he enters the kitchen, hair mussed.

"Pancakes!" Giovanni wriggles and I let him down to repeat his ridiculously affectionate small animal act with my brother.

Our gazes meet over Giovanni's head, and I read in Sev's face what I'm sure is on my face too. Bemusement. Love. Disbelief that we're this lucky.

Sev, Vito, and I bought this chalet a few years ago and have spent nearly every holiday here since. Christmas, birthdays, summer holidays. There's always an excuse to get together.

"The girls are watching cartoons in the snug," Sev tells Giovanni as he puts him down. "Why don't you go and join them?"

My son rushes off and I flip a pancake onto the stack, before pouring a new one.

"Those girls," I say. "Might need to check on them." Because Ella and my twin daughters and their cousins are thick as thieves. Trouble. "Happy birthday."

"Thanks. You look old. You seen Vito?" Sev pours coffee from the pot I've made into two mugs. Still makes me smile when I make a cafetiere of coffee. Every day.

"He's still in bed with his wife, as far as I know."

Sev rolls his eyes. "I'll be back in a minute."

That's about as demonstrative as he gets, but I don't care. We're still brothers, and rivals, and our families get on brilliantly. I see how he is with his wife and all the kids, and I know he doesn't need to be huggy with me. He has lots of physical touch and emotional connection with his wife and all the kids.

Sev is stupidly in love with his wife. Waits on her hand and foot, so I know without asking that when he leaves the kitchen, he's going to take her coffee. Then he might return to help me, or more likely go and check in with the kids.

The cosy domesticity of it all is charming and yet, if you'd told me before that fateful day that I discovered Ella in the office that I'd be this happy, and have a big secure, happy family, and my kids would have cousins to play with? Pah. I'd have never believed you.

But here we are.

"That smells delicious." Ella wraps her arms around my waist, and I startle before relaxing into her embrace. Her bump nestles on the top of my buttocks.

My pregnant wife.

"All for you, sweet one." I say that the reason I make pancakes is for me, but it's Ella who really loves them. Sugar, lemon, chocolate sauce, and maple syrup, I always ensure there are all her favourites, even when it's my birthday. Reaching around, I get Ella in front of me, and the stove with the cooking pancakes to the side, and kiss her.

She responds by pressing herself to me, and my body reacts in the way it always does to my wife. Oh god, she's so perfect.

"You'll give me a hard-on," I growl into her ear.

"Oh no, what a terrible thing," she replies, deadpan. "You might give me another baby." She smirks.

"Do not tempt me." I sweep my hand over her hair. "We have to have a nice family breakfast, and now I'm going to be thinking about filling you with sperm and how gorgeous you are pregnant." I kiss her again, deeply, inhaling her goodness. I want to eat her up, like the best pancake ever.

My family is everything to me, but my wife is the centre of it all. My rock, my sunshine dragon. All I could ever need.

I said as many children as my wife would allow me, and that has turned out to be four, and one more on the way.

So far.

"This afternoon, Ella, I'm going to get the kids off and entertained with their cousins. And then I want a birthday present from you."

I draw back and look into those hazel eyes of hers, gold flecks sparkling in the morning light.

"My love." Her voice is patient. "What makes you think I haven't already planned that?"

EXTENDED EPILOGUE
RAFE

6 years later, that afternoon

Ella is too tired to go to the amusement park that afternoon, and feels faint.

Sev's wife insists that I should stay home with her while all the kids go with her, Sev, Vito, and his wife. And while Vito gives me a dirty look, he melts under his wife's gentle arm tug.

Honestly, Ella is a genius. Executed with finesse and accuracy, by one pm she has arranged it so we have the whole house to ourselves.

We sate our initial lust with a quick fuck in the lounge, on the sofa, her riding me, me encouraging.

Being pregnant makes my wife horny, and unable to be under me, and I'm absolutely fine to assist from any angle she likes. Behind is a favourite for us both, but I don't mind so long as I get to watch her come.

I've laid down special throws so we can be as messy as we like, and while I tell her she has to keep every bit inside her, gravity has a way of thwarting us.

"So fatigued," I tease her as we lie on the sofa in the sunshine, rubbing her back. She's full of my semen again, and fuck I love the way I can see it seeping out from between her legs.

"Yep. Want a drink?"

I laugh as she springs up, hand over her pussy to prevent the otherwise inevitable drips.

"I'll go," I offer, but Ella has already waddled off—perfectly naked—to the kitchen.

Reclining on the soft throw, I watch her. When she's not pregnant, she'd return with champagne. But of course, she returns with coffee.

"Decaf?"

She nods and smiles and my heart, already so much mush, melts. I love her excessively. I push up into a sitting position.

"Put them down, sweet one. It's not coffee I need right now."

Her eyes go wide.

"Come here."

She saunters to me, hips swaying, two cups in her hands. But I'm not looking at the coffee. I'm watching her breasts. They're bigger since her pregnancies.

"Mm. You're so gorgeous."

I let her put the cups down onto the side table, but as soon as she's within arm's reach, I get my hands on her waist, and smooth over her bump. It's small now, but it suits her. It always does.

"You're just silly about the baby," she laughs.

"I'm silly about *you*, you when pregnant, *and* our children."

"I love you," she says, a soft smile on her face. A hint of insecurity I hadn't even noticed dissipates.

I tilt my head, and grab her hand, pulling her down. "What is it, beautiful?"

"Nothing!"

"Did you really think I only love our babies?"

"No!"

Maybe not, but maybe for a moment? Perhaps a tiny bit? Ella has been a young mother. I sometimes forget how young she is, given how much has happened. Four children, one more on the way. A mafia to run, with all the risks and rewards that involves. She's brave and capable, and cares for our children.

"What about you, huh?" I shift my feet apart and gently turn her in my arms and draw her to sit, her back to my chest. "Maybe you need to be just you and me for a moment. My naughty girl."

She leans into me, and I press my face into her neck, breathing in her scent.

"Spread your legs."

And my good girl doesn't hesitate. The trust is as sweet and strong a drug as caffeine, and just as addictive. My cock is solid as she exposes herself. I can't see it, but I bet my seed is seeping out of her. I run my hands over her silky inner thighs.

"Touch yourself."

She reaches down and slides her fingers between her legs, and I purr with approval as she snuggles back into me and sighs with pleasure.

We don't do this often. Normally I lick her, or finger her, or more usually she comes on my cock.

I see her hand movements adjust as she starts to tease her clit.

"That's it. My good girl. It's still sensitive after you came earlier, isn't it?"

"Mmmhum." She nods.

"Make yourself come for me, and then I'll fuck you."

In truth, I already could. We both know it, because my cock is pressed into her back. Hard. Again.

She shifts, rubbing herself into me, as though to make exactly this point, and I grasp her thighs in retaliation.

"I'll take you from behind this time, beautiful girl. Make sure I ram into you hard so our baby knows how much their daddy loves you."

She whimpers and her hand speeds up.

"How many times can I make you come this afternoon, huh? Our dirty little secret while the kids are off having a nice time without us."

She writhes, pressing into my cock. I circle my hips, showing her how much I want her and getting just a bit of sensation on my cock.

"I'm going to fuck you so hard, sunshine dragon, I'm going to rail you over this sofa, right here in the sunshine," I say into her ear, leaning over her to see her touching herself. I still have her thighs pinned, and there's something delicious about the sight of her soft flesh held down.

Her pert little tits are right there, and my mouth waters to take one in my mouth. She's so sweet and ripe, even more so now than when we first met.

"I'm sorely tempted to turn you over and get you onto my cock, Ella, I really am."

She nods and whines incoherently, beginning to shake with the need to come.

But I like this moment of restraint. I push down on her legs to emphasise my point. "I'm not sure you even remember how to make yourself come now, do you?"

She sobs, and that rather proves my point.

"Fuck, sunshine dragon, I love spoiling you. I love

eating your pussy until you scream. I love being balls deep inside you. Make yourself come, and I'll do it for you three times more."

She's not quite there, and now it's a matter of principle that I don't help her, however much I long to feel her break apart. And however much I need to taste her gorgeous breasts.

"Pinch your nipples," I growl, and satisfy myself for now with kissing her neck and enjoying the view as she does as I tell her. "That's it. Until it almost hurts, the way you like it."

She keens, frustrated.

"So close, aren't you?" I kiss up to her ear and lick the sensitive skin there before nibbling at her earlobe, making her shudder.

"That's it. It'll be so much easier when I'm inside your body. I can't get enough of you, wife. I love you so much. And you're gorgeous pregnant, or full of my cock, or covered with my come. I want it dripping out of you."

Her movements are frantic now.

"That's it. Make yourself come and I'll satisfy you properly. I'll stuff you with cock. I'll breed you all over again."

And though we both know I can't breed her when she's obviously already pregnant with my child, that does it.

She jerks and cries out, arching against me.

"Well done," I soothe. "You're doing so well. So beautiful when you come like this. Lovely."

But even as I praise her, I let go of her thighs and reach down for my boxers. It's the work of a second to release my cock.

She's still coming, boneless and shaking as I wrap my arms around her and pull her up my chest.

I don't ask. We're so far beyond that now, I'm certain

she's as eager as I am. I can feel it, knowing her body as well as I know my own. I grasp my cock and notch the head at her soaked entrance, and thrust up into her.

She chokes, and immediately I feel the hot wet sheath of her pulse as she comes again, or maybe just clenches in another wave.

Flexing up until I hit the top of her, the head of my cock is cupped deliciously by her tightness.

"Use me," she pants, and I don't need telling twice.

I grab her like the doll she is compared to my hulking self, and lift her up, only to pull her down, hard.

I groan as she screams.

It's not a bad noise though. It's pure pleasure. I do it again. And again. Faster, deeper.

"You're heaven on my cock," I manage to grind out the praise. She needs to hear it, and I need to say it. "You're being such a good girl for me."

It's my favourite thing, praising my girl. It's like even after years, we both need to make up for the eighteen months when I didn't tell her how good she was, how much I loved her, how she completed me. It's over the top, but I feel like I can never tell her enough that she's perfect. So even as I take her, bouncing her on my lap as I thrust up into her, I whisper filthy words of love.

"Please breed me," she murmurs, arching into me.

My balls tingle. Fuck, she knows what that does to me. It's nonsensical, she's already pregnant, but that is beside the point.

"Say it again, louder, and I will."

"Breed me."

"Scream it." Pleasure builds at the base of my spine and my cock swells further inside of her, like I'm trying to reach up as far as possible.

"Breed me!" she yells it and I slam her down onto my cock as I come so hard all I can think of is her and me, and the places we're joined. The way we are together.

I jerk and shudder and empty myself into Ella. I give her everything I have, draining my balls in spurt after spurt deep inside my wife. Then I collapse, and pull her onto me, her back snug to my chest, still joined.

"My best girl," I tell her. "My sweetest, sexiest, best love. I adore you so much, Ella."

She purrs contentedly and turns her head for a kiss. "I love you too. My blue alien husband."

THANKS

Thank you for reading, I hope you enjoyed it.

Want to read a little more Happily Ever After? Click to get exclusive epilogues and free stories! or head to Evie-RoseAuthor.com

If you have a moment, I'd really appreciate a review wherever you like to talk about books. Reviews, however brief, help readers find stories they'll love.

Love to get the news first? Follow me on your favored social media platform - I love to chat to readers and you get all the latest gossip.

If the newsletter is too much like commitment, I recommend following me on BookBub, where you'll just get new release notifications and deals.

- amazon.com/author/evierose
- bookbub.com/authors/evie-rose
- instagram.com/evieroseauthor
- tiktok.com/@EvieRoseAuthor

INSTALOVE BY EVIE ROSE

Mafia Boss Marriage

Owned by her Enemy

I didn't expect the ruthless new kingpin—an older man, gorgeous and hard—to extract such a price for a ceasefire: an arranged marriage.

Kingpin's Baby

I beg the Kingpin for help... And he offers marriage.

Grumpy Bosses

Older Hotter Grumpier

My billionaire boss catches me reading when I should be working. And the punishment...?

Everyone is Watching

His Public Claim

My innocence is up for auction, sold to the highest bidder.

Marrying the Boss

Baby Proposal

My boss walked in on me buying "magic juice" online... And now he's demanding to be my baby's daddy!

London Mafia Bosses

Captured by the Mafia Boss

I might be an innocent runaway, but I'm at my friend's funeral to avenge her murder by the mafia boss: King.

Taken by the Kingpin

Tall, dark, older and dangerous, I shouldn't want him.

I thought my mafia connections were in the past, and I was alone. But powerful mafia boss Sebastian Laurent hasn't forgotten me.

Stolen by the Mafia King

I didn't know he has been watching me all this time.

I had a plan to escape. Everything is going perfectly at my wedding rehearsal dinner until *he* turns up.

Caught by the Kingpin

The kingpin growls a warning that I shouldn't try his patience by attempting to escape.

There's no way I'm staying as his little prisoner.

Claimed by the Mobster

I'm in love with my ex-boyfriend's dad: a dangerous and powerful mafia boss twice my age.

Snatched by the Bratva

I have an excruciating crush on this man who comes into the coffee shop. Every day. He's older, gorgeous, perfectly dressed. He has a Russian accent and silver eyes.

Kidnapped by the Mafia Boss

I locked myself in the bathroom when my date pulled out a knife. Then a tall dark rescuer crashed through the door... and kidnapped me.

Held by the Bratva

"Who hurt you?"

Before I know it, my gorgeous neighbour has scooped me up into his arms and taken me to his penthouse. And he won't let me go.

Filthy Scottish Kingpins

Forbidden Appeal

He's older and rich, and my teenage crush re-surfaces as I beg the former kingpin to help me escape a mafia arranged marriage. He stares at me like I'm a temptress he wants to banish, but we're snowed in at his Scottish castle.

Captive Desires

I was sent to kill him, but he's captured me, and I'm at his mercy. He says he'll let me go if I beg him to take his...